RICHARD ARMSTRONG

Sea change

D1364466

 KNIGHT BOOKS

the paperback division of Brockhampton Press

SBN 340 04199 4

*This edition first published 1969 by Knight Books,
the paperback division of Brockhampton Press Ltd, Leicester*

*Printed and bound in Great Britain by
Cox & Wyman Ltd, London, Reading and Fakenham*

First published by J. M. Dent & Sons Ltd 1948

1

WHEN Cam Renton joined the *Langdale* in Liverpool he was just turned sixteen. He was a tall lad for his age and at first glance seemed slightly built; but his height concealed a big-boned frame and already there was about him a hint of wiry strength, particularly in the set of his shoulders and the size of his hands.

His face, like his body, was long and lean. Normally it was a quiet face which broke easily into a gap-toothed grin, but as he trudged along the dockside that blazing July afternoon, his wide mouth was sullen and a vague doubt clouded his deep-set eyes.

Cam had always been keen on the sea, and when he joined his first ship a few days after his fifteenth birthday his future seemed to run straight and clear. Before him lay a four-year apprenticeship; four years of study and practice in seamanship and navigation and a second mate's certificate at the end of it; then a junior officer's berth while he put in his time and sat in turn for mate, master, and extra-master, and finally command of his own ship. He had started full of enthusiasm, but somehow it hadn't worked out as he expected. One year of the four was already gone and he felt it had brought him no nearer to his goal, for though he had learned much about the sea and the way of ships none of it seemed very important. And now with his second deep-water voyage over and his third about to begin, there was no more eagerness in him and he was unsure both of himself and what he wanted to do.

He spotted the ship across the dock and set down his suitcase to stare at her. She lay sandwiched between the great round stern of a transatlantic liner and the flaring bow of an Australian mail packet. The giants dwarfed her, but in spite of that she looked well enough to be proud of, and at the sight of her Cam's face lit up. She was a single-screw steamer carrying just on eight thousand tons. Her paint was spotless, and above the varnished teakwood rail of her upper bridge the telegraphs and binnacle top flashed back the sun like mirrors.

'Not a bad-looking old wagon, at that,' he said to himself grudgingly, and for a moment he seemed to shed his dejection. Then he remembered his last ship. She, too, had been a decent-looking wagon, but that hadn't got him anywhere. His mouth went grim again, and picking up his grip, he continued along the wall.

The *Langdale* was loading for Barbados and a string of ports along the Spanish Main. Abreast of her the dock was littered with cargo – bales, crates, and cases, each item with the port of destination stencilled on it. Dodging the sweating stevedores and swinging slings, Cam read the names as he passed. There was stuff for Barbados, Port of Spain, Curaçao, and half a dozen other places vaguely remembered from history and geography lessons – and against his will he felt his interest in the voyage quicken at the sudden thought that it would make these far-off ports real to him.

Reaching the gangway at last, he climbed its steep slope and stood at the head of it looking down on the ship.

Her decks were piled high with stores, which some of the crew were sorting, checking, and stowing away. There were carcasses of beef and mutton, cases of tinned food, sacks of vegetables, casks of oil, drums of paint, coils of wire and manilla rope, and all the odds and ends needed to maintain a ship and feed her crew for a third of a year.

Staring curiously at these men who were to be his shipmates for the next four months or longer, Cam picked out the second mate, a junior engineer, and the cook, then his roving glance rested on a short, thickset youngster of about his own age who leaned against the galley door mopping his face with a grimy handkerchief. He wore a blue boiler suit and a battered badge cap was stuck on the back of his tangle of carroty hair. Cam crossed the deck towards him.

'I'm Renton, the new apprentice,' he said. 'They told me there'd be two of us and I suppose you're the other?'

The carroty-haired lad levered himself upright and eyed Cam warily. He had a queer little habit of screwing up his face until his eyes were half closed, then shooting out a mouthful of words as if there were pressure behind them. 'That's right,' he popped. 'Roberts is my name but everybody calls me Rusty. What did you say yours was?'

'Renton. Cam Renton.' Cam grinned. 'It's really Campbell but the last bit got lost a long time ago. Where's our room, and is the skipper aboard?'

Rusty held up his hand. 'Now hold on a bit. I'll show you our quarters, but what do you want with the skipper for Pete's sake?'

'Well, my orders are to report to him – Captain Carey, isn't it?'

'That's right.' Rusty yanked open a teakwood door just abaft the galley and led the way along a short alleyway. 'But forget it, brother. Old Ma Carey won't mean much in your life. It's the mate you want. He runs this ship and whatever you do don't make any mistake about that. Here we are!' He flung open another door and waved his hand. 'Here's the happy home. Messroom next door, bath at the end of the alley-way.'

Cam stepped inside the cabin and dropped his suitcase, then

7

looked around. It was a fair-sized place with two bunks built in one above the other. There was a large chest of drawers and a washstand with a tip-up basin, a mirror and little racks for tooth glasses and water bottle. Above the chest was a bookshelf and a cushioned locker ran at right angles to the bunks. Between the lockers and the washstand a handy little table was screwed to the bulkhead.

'A bit of all right, isn't it?' said Rusty.

Cam dropped into the corner of the locker and leaned back. 'Oh,' he said gloomily, 'I suppose it's not bad.'

Rusty's face screwed up. 'Not bad!' he exploded, waving his hand at the two outsize ports above the bunks, the gleaming mahogany furniture, and spotless white-painted bulkheads. 'Not bad! Crikey, you should see some of the dog-holes apprentices have to live in. Why, man, this is . . .' Then suddenly aware that everything was not as it should be he turned and stared at his new room-mate. 'What's up?' he demanded.

Cam stretched out a long leg and stared at the toe of his shoe. 'Tell me one thing. Which watch are you in – the mate's or second mate's?'

Rusty flushed under his freckles. 'Well, to tell the truth I haven't been in a watch yet.'

'How long have you been in the ship then?'

'Two voyages.'

Cam stood up and kicked savagely at his suitcase. 'Two voyages on day work and you ask me what's up. I'm sick of it, if you want to know.'

'But why? What's wrong?'

For a moment Cam stared out through the porthole at the bustle on the dock wall, then suddenly he swung round. 'Everything's wrong,' he said. 'Just everything. I don't know how you're fixed or how much you care, but this business of

8

going to sea means something to me. I started with a whole lot of ideas and a plan. I wanted to learn. I wanted a second mate's ticket; I wanted to get on to the bridge and do things. And what's happened? I've spent a year – a quarter of my apprenticeship – polishing brass, chipping rust, and slapping paint on bulkheads, and so far as being a deck officer goes, I'm just where I started. Now I'm in for another voyage of it and you ask me what's wrong!'

'But that's all part of the job, isn't it?' objected Rusty.

'A deck-hand's job, yes. But I'm not a deck-hand and don't want to be one. I'm an apprentice, serving my time and learning to be an officer. I want to learn navigation and seamanship; I want to stand a watch and get to know the rule of the road, how to handle a ship.' He paused. 'How long have you been at sea?'

Rusty made a calculation on his fingers. 'Fourteen months.'

'And have you stood a watch yet or done a trick at the wheel or a look-out? Have you handled a sextant or laid off a course on a chart? Not on your life. I bet you've chipped rust and cleaned brass all the time.'

'Well!' Rusty's voice was defensive. 'I've learned to steer in the dog-watches and I can box the compass and drive a winch.'

'And that's all. And let me tell you this, it's all you will do if I know anything. Don't you see it; doesn't it make you mad?'

Rusty shuffled his feet. 'I'd never thought of it that way. But it does seem a bit rough.' He frowned. 'In any case there's not much we can do about it, is there?'

'We can raise a stink with the mate.'

'Fat lot of good that will do. Wait till you see him!'

Cam turned to the door. 'I'm going to do that now. Where's he likely to be?'

'In the saloon, checking bills of lading. You don't mean you're going to ask him to put us on watches? He'll chase you for your life.'

Cam set his jaw. 'I don't care. I've had enough of being messed about! And I want to know where I stand from the first.'

A couple of minutes later he was standing outside the saloon entrance, his heart beating just a little bit faster than usual, but his mind firmly made up that whatever sort of man this mate might be he would have a showdown with him.

'Anyway,' he said to himself, taking a jerk at his uniform jacket, 'whatever he is, he can't eat me; he can only bawl me out and I can stand that okay.' Then he tapped at the door and stepped over the coaming.

There was only one man in the saloon and the three tarnished gold bands on the cuff of his old coat told Cam this was the mate.

He was an extraordinary figure, little more than five feet high, and the enormous breadth of his shoulders made him seem even shorter than that. His chest was like a barrel and the hands with which he sorted the pile of papers before him seemed as big as soup plates, the fingers like bunches of bananas. His head was small and round, covered with wiry hair cropped close and standing up all over it like the bristles on a brush. It was set on a thin, scraggy neck, dark with sun and weatherbeat, and as he turned to stare at Cam it jerked forward with a comical movement, stretching out from the huge shoulders like an old tortoise peering out of its shell.

His face was the next shock. Unlike the wrinkled neck, it was as smooth as a boy's and tanned to coffee colour. The nose was big and hooked like the beak of a bird of prey, the mouth straight and so thin-lipped it was no more than a line on his face. The eyes, deep-set under shaggy brows, were blue and hard and cold as chips of ice.

He looked at Cam for quite half a minute without speaking and when at last he did so, his voice was the final shock.

'Well?' he said. Just that one word, but instead of being roared or snapped out, it came gently, hardly more than a whisper.

'My name is Renton, sir,' said Cam. 'I'm the new apprentice and I was told to report to Captain Carey.'

The cold blue eyes moved down from the boy's face to his feet, then slowly travelled up again. 'First voyage?'

'No, sir. I've done two trips in the *Styhead*.'

'Okay. Get your dunnage aboard this afternoon and turn to with the bosun in the morning. I'll have a word with him about you.' He waved his hand towards the door and turned back to his papers.

Cam clutched at his courage and swallowed hard.

'Excuse me, sir, but . . .'

The mate did not look up. 'All right, lad,' he said irritably. 'I'm busy now. Off you go. Young Roberts will show you round and put you wise.'

Still Cam stood his ground. 'But I wanted to speak to you, sir.'

The mate's hands came down on the papers and his head shot out as he looked up. The cold blue eyes bored into Cam's and he stared back manfully.

'Well?' the husky voice whispered again.

'It's like this, sir. I want to know where I stand.'

'About what?'

'About work and all that. You see, sir, I . . .' Cam hesitated.

'Yes, yes. Go on.'

Cam gulped. 'Well sir, I've done a year of my time and I don't think I'm being treated right. I came to sea to serve my time, not to work with the bosun. Anybody can chip rust and polish brass. I want to learn things, things that matter, like navigation. I want –'

'Enough!' The mate's voice remained a whisper but there was something in the way he said the word that stopped Cam like a slap in the face. 'Now listen to this carefully. The work aboard this ship is my responsibility. It's my job to decide what you do and your place is to do it. The one thing I won't tolerate is a sea-lawyer. Understand?'

The colour had drained from the boy's face.

'Understand?' the mate repeated.

'I think I do, sir, but –'

'There aren't any buts about it. You'll turn to with the bosun in the morning. Now scram.'

For a moment Cam hesitated, but already the mate was absorbed in his papers again and at last, with a white set face, he turned away and leaving the saloon went back to the cabin in the starboard alley-way.

Rusty was waiting for him. 'Well?' he demanded. 'Is it to be watches?'

Cam jerked off his cap and flung it savagely into the top bunk. 'No, it's not, and so far as I can see it never will be. What's eating the old coot, anyway? I tried to speak reasonably to him. Is he always like that?'

'You mean snappy and tough? Always. He's a queer old chap and sometimes I think he's a bit gone in the lid.' Rusty tapped his forehead significantly. 'He's an old sailing-ship man and maybe he doesn't go much on the seamen of today.'

Cam dropped into the corner of the settee. 'But it's not good enough. What's he think we are anyhow and how does he get away with it?'

Rusty sat up with a jerk. 'Ask anybody in Liverpool about Anderson of the *Langdale* and they'll tell you. Look at the ship. There isn't a better-kept wagon in the port. And he's a wizard with cargo. All the claims against the ship for lost packages, broached cases, and over-carried consignments don't amount to more than chicken-feed in half a dozen voyages. And the crew! The *Langdale*'s no yacht but her crowd couldn't be paid to leave her. It's not the ship, but Andy. They'd sail with him on a raft, for they think there never was a mate to touch him.'

Cam got up and moved restlessly round the room. The colour was back in his face now and there was a hard fighting gleam in his eyes.

'But,' he protested, 'how does he expect us to learn anything? Three more years, then we have an examination to sit.'

'I know. I know.' Rusty's freckled face was puckered with worry. 'But moaning about it doesn't make it any easier. I've had two voyages with him and I know it's no good kicking. He's mate and that's that. He has his own way of doing things – even handling apprentices – and we've got to put up with it.'

'Well, I won't!'

'It's easy to say that, but what can you do?'

Cam's jaw thrust out. 'I'll complain to the skipper or write to the owners, or –' he stopped as a new thought struck him '– or I'll sling my hand in. For two pins I'd do just that.'

Rusty jumped up. 'Sling your hand in! You mean walk ashore and not come back? Not sail? I thought you said you were keen on going to sea, that it meant something to you?'

Cam turned towards the port and felt the sun-warmed breeze that came gently through it on to his face, and suddenly his nose was full of the smell of the ship and the sea – paint and tar and new-sawn timber, the heady scent of hot sugar and the reek of hides. He heard the clatter of winches, the quick stamp of busy feet, and all the lesser sounds of the work that would go on without stopping now until in a few short hours the mooring lines would be slipped and the *Langdale* pulled out on her voyage.

The voyage! Strange seas; misty loom of lonely headlands; sun and sparkle and tumbling clouds; green jewels of islands and the channels between them first ploughed by the keels of Drake's little ships in search of the stately galleons of Spain; and the ports – Barbados and Trinidad, La Guayra and Curaçao.

Then Rusty was speaking again.

'You know, brother,' he popped earnestly, 'you can't do that. Besides, you never know. Maybe when we've cleared away he will put us on watches. But in any case, you can't sling your hand in like that!'

Cam stared out through the port. Of course he couldn't. It was too much to give up, and besides, how could he admit defeat? Other fellows went through with it and got by. Why shouldn't he?

He flung round impatiently. 'Oh, forget it, Rusty. I was just hearing myself talk. We'll wait to see what happens.'

Rusty's puckered face relaxed. 'That's the stuff. I'll have to get out on deck again or the old blighter will be chasing me. Maybe I'll get knocked off about four and we'll be able to get the rest of your gear down together.' He paused in the doorway. 'See you soon.'

'Okay.' Cam grinned and waved his hand.

But alone again, he returned to his brooding, and once more the shadows of unrest and uncertainty were in his eyes.

2

WITH Rusty's help, Cam Renton got his big sea-bag aboard after tea, and the rest of the evening they spent settling in.

The first step towards this was to share out the drawers and hanging space in the wardrobe, and the second to get all Rusty's gear into his own territory. This last was quite a job, for Rusty had been on his own for a whole voyage and had spread himself all over the cabin. It was done at last, however, and then Cam began to unpack his bag and his suit-case, stowing each item as he took it out.

There was a lot of stuff – shore-going clothes, overalls, and tough-wearing togs for working in; light cotton shirts and shorts for the tropics; and all the bulky gear such as oilskins and seaboots and long thick woollen stockings for hard weather. Finally there were the odds and ends he had collected in his first few months at sea – a sail-maker's palm and a little box of needles, a sheath-knife, books on navigation, meteorology, and seamanship, and, greatest treasure of all, a battered old sextant he had seen in a junk shop and saved a whole voyage to buy.

When all the clothes were put away, the books stowed on the shelf, and the sextant set in its wooden case squarely on top of the chest of drawers, they tossed for choice of bunks. Cam won and without hesitation took the top one, for this would give him the portlight just by his head.

Rusty was very pleased to have someone of his own age with him again, and while they worked he chattered about the ship and her crew to such good purpose that, by the time everything was squared up, Cam felt he knew all there was to know about both. Moreover, his worry about the future, the flare-up with the mate, all the uneasiness he had felt earlier in the day, were driven right out of his mind and he began to feel excited about the voyage.

There was still a glimmer of daylight in the sky when they turned in, but they lay for a long time swopping yarns and getting to know each other. It was far past midnight when Cam switched off the light and settled down, and then somehow for him sleep would not come. His worry flooded back on him and he found himself thinking of the fierce little man he had met in the saloon; going over their brief encounter time and time again, and wondering uneasily if he had made a mistake, and if so how it would affect his life and work aboard the *Langdale*.

What if he had gone off half-cocked about the mate and watches? What if he had put his foot in it and made an enemy before he had been half an hour aboard her? There was no denying old Andy was a queer figure – almost frightening with his huge hands and immense shoulders and little husky voice; but was any one of those things, or all of them put together and his anger thrown in, any real reason for disliking him? After all, Cam told himself, the mate of a ship is a busy man; all the responsibility for cargo and stores and crew falls on him, and that's more than enough to make anybody a bit ratty at being interrupted.

On the other hand there was his order for Cam to turn to with the bosun, and the fact that in two voyages Rusty hadn't yet been in a watch. It didn't look too hopeful.

Cam turned uneasily and stared out through the porthole across the deserted dock wall.

Of course, his thoughts ran on, he might be all wrong. Maybe he was getting things out of proportion and seeing the whole business lopsided. There was one very good reason he could think of for Rusty never having been in a watch. With less than a year of his time served he couldn't take the place of an A.B., and to put him in one watch as an extra hand would be unfair to the other, beside upsetting the whole routine of wheels and look-outs.

That must be it. This voyage, with two of them aboard, there would be an apprentice for each watch and everything would be fair and even. No doubt old Andy would be giving them their orders about it next day. Perhaps he'd already fixed it with the bosun and he would be rousing them out bright and early to turn to with the hands and they'd quickly be in the thick of all the bustle and excitement.

At this point Cam relaxed. Everything was going to be all right. Rusty seemed a decent sort of bloke, the *Langdale* was a good ship, the voyage everything anybody could wish for, and it was time he snapped out of his moping mood.

He fell asleep on this thought and it was still there right in front of his mind when he woke next morning.

It was the bosun himself who called the boys. He was a wiry little Irishman with a dark Celtic face and a great bull's roar of a voice, which croaked like an old frog's when he tried to speak softly and boomed from one end of the ship to the other when he let it go. For the deck crew he was, next to the mate, the most important man aboard. The mate had the responsibility of deciding what should be done and when, but it was the bosun who saw it done and decided how. For this he needed to be, apart from the mate, the best seaman in the ship and he had to be able to hold the men together as a team and get the best out of each of them as well.

'Come on, my brave boyos!' he croaked. 'Show a leg!'

'What's the time?' yawned Rusty.

'It's quarter to six and the orders are all hands to turn to

17

at six and get the old hooker ready for sea. We're sailing on the afternoon tide and there's a devil of a lot to do.' The bosun turned to Cam, who had already swung his legs over the bunkboard and was rubbing the sleep out of his eyes. 'You're young Renton, eh?'

Cam shot out on to the deck and grinned. 'That's right. Did the mate say which watches we were to go in or shall we toss for it?'

The bosun pushed back his battered felt hat and scratched his head. 'I don't know anything about watches. All he said was you were to turn to with the hands. You'd better see him about that yourself after breakfast.' The keen brown eyes in his thin face measured Cam carefully, then his hard brown hand shot out and touched him lightly on the shoulder. 'Okay, son. There's coffee in the galley to jolt the dregs of sleep out of your mind. Nip into your duds and get along before it's all gone.' He strode across the room to the door. 'And see that carrot-topped partner of yours doesn't drop off again. He'd sleep through three hurricanes and a Donnybrook fair, if you let him,' he croaked, then he was gone.

But for once Rusty was wide awake. Tumbling out of his bunk, he straightened himself in a series of quick jerks, then stretched. 'Looks like another voyage on day work for us,' he yawned.

Cam lifted his face out of the wash basin and groped for the towel. 'Maybe not. We'd better give old Andy a chance. He's got a lot more on his mind than you and me, you know.'

Rusty stuck his head in the bowl, then came up for breath. 'But the bosun said –'

'I know.' Cam flushed as he wriggled into his boiler suit. 'I know. But look, Rusty, I talked a lot of tripe yesterday. Let's forget it and start afresh. I'll try him again after breakfast like the bosun said.'

18

'Okay by me, brother, and whichever way it goes I'm easy. I don't mind day work – every evening free and all night in your bunk. You started the moan.'

'Right then, leave it at that.' Cam jerked his cap off the peg. 'I'm off for that coffee. You'd better get a wiggle on.'

When he reached the galley Cam found the whole deck crew there before him, and as he sipped the scalding black coffee he eyed them curiously. There were ten men all told and although many days had still to pass before he knew them all as individuals, he was able right from the start to divide them into groups.

The bosun he had aleady met, but now he saw him again standing alongside the other petty officer – the carpenter – who was a Scandinavian called Rasmussen. He was a giant of a man with hands almost as big as Andy's, and gentle blue eyes which seemed to be looking at something far away that only himself could see. He was always referred to as 'Chippy.'

The remainder of the men were A.B.s and they divided into three lots – the mate's watch, the second mate's watch, and the day gang; three and three and two.

Normally the mate's watch was responsible for the fore-deck and fo'c's'le head and the second mate's for the after deck and poop; but on sailing day, with all the hatches to batten down and the whole ship to square up for sea, the deck crew worked as one gang.

They started forrard with the general idea of working gradually towards the poop, leaving everything shipshape behind them as they went, and Cam found himself paired off with one of the sailors in the second mate's watch – a tall man with a long mournful face and brown eyes, sad like a spaniel's. His name was Calshot and partly because of his appearance and partly because of his habit of foreseeing disaster in every-thing, he was nicknamed 'Calamity.' To Calshot a rain squall was always the forerunner of a gale, and a gale the advance guard of a hurricane; he saw in every little cut or graze the possibility of amputation and lockjaw, and a slight headache for him could be nothing but the first sign of yellow fever or bubonic plague.

When Cam saw the fore-deck he wondered how they would ever get the mess cleared up at all, let alone in time to sail with the tide just after noon. The last of the cargo had come aboard late the previous night and the stevedores had done no more than spread a tarpaulin over each hatch, slinging a few hatch boards on any old how to hold it. They had left the derricks swinging and the decks were littered with hatch beams, battens and boards, derrick guys and tackles, odds and ends of slings and cargo hooks, and fathom after fathom of wire runner twisting this way and that way from the gin blocks on the derrick heads and the heel blocks at the foot of the mast.

But the bosun seemed to take it all as a matter of course. He led them to it step by step, as if each little job were separate from the rest and nothing else counted.

They started on number one hatch and the first thing to be done was to strip it. When the tarpaulin had been hauled off and the odd hatch boards thrown clear, it was revealed as a great rectangular hole in the deck, thirty feet long and twenty-five across. To make the ship seaworthy this had to be covered in such a way that it wouldn't only be watertight but also strong enough to withstand the weight of big seas breaking on it.

First the great steel thwartship beams, each weighing over a ton, were swung up by winch and dropped into the sockets in the hatch coamings. There were three of these and each was bolted into place by the carpenter. Next came the fore-and-afters, which were three heavy baulks of timber laid evenly spaced at right angles across the beams. These carried the hatch boards – eight-foot lengths of pitch-pine, two and a half inches thick, fitted with a scooped-out handhold at each end – which lay athwart the fore-and-afters in three lines. Handling these was the heaviest job of all. Each of them carried two numbers, one indicating the tier it belonged to and the other its place in the tier, and they had to be yanked out of the raffle on the deck, swung up on to the hatch, and dropped into place all by sheer muscle power.

While the beams and fore-and-afters were being dealt with, Cam had time to look around and notice things. He saw the sun, like a flat disk and blood-red, pushing up through the faint mist that lay low over the roofs of the warehouses; he felt and enjoyed the freshness of the morning and the strange hush and stillness of it on which the bosun's voice boomed like the deep notes of an organ; he saw odd little things about the men – that Calamity Calshot was so tall and thin he bent over at the top, that everything about him drooped, his moustache, his shoulders, his mouth, and his long nose; that the carpenter whistled through his teeth as he worked and always the same few notes of the same song, as if he was trying to remember it and never could; he saw the blood go out of the sun as it came clear of the mist, and the mist itself turn into a haze that spilled across the ridge tiles of the dock buildings and touched everything with gold. But when they started on the hatch boards he had to give all his mind as well as his energy to the job of keeping up with Calamity.

After the hatch boards came the tarpaulins. There were three of them, each spread separately and carefully tucked into the cleats that were riveted to the coaming at intervals of about a foot all round, eight inches below the edge. Then the battens – long strips of steel about two and a half inches wide – were dropped into place and a hard-wood wedge

21

pushed into every cleat. Lastly the carpenter went round with his heavy hammer, and when he had belted each wedge up solid, the hatch was ready to face any normal hazard of the sea and a whole lot more maybe.

The next thing was the derricks. There were four of these at number one hatch – two stepped at the foot of the foremast and two on samson posts at the break of the fo'c's'le head. They swung on swivelled pins called goosenecks and each of them carried what seemed to be an amazing tangle of gear. There was the topping-lift, which was a heavy tackle shackled one end to the head of the derrick, the other to the cross-trees of the mast or an eyebolt in the top of the samson post. This raised the derrick to the proper angle for working. Then came the guys – two to each derrick – lighter tackles fastened to tails spliced into the head. The gin block at the head of the derrick and the heel block at the foot of the mast completed the rig. The derricks had to be lowered into their crutches and lashed there, then all these ropes and wires and blocks and tackles dismantled, coiled down, and stowed away in the bosun's locker.

Everything went without a hitch and by half past eight when they knocked off for breakfast the fore-deck was finished. Cam looked back on it from the top of the bridge-deck ladder with a little thrill of pride. They had certainly done a good job, and he knew by the sting in his hands and the ache across his shoulders that he had pulled his weight with the best of them. Calamity, however, was determined to see something sinister even in the progress they had made.

'Don't kid yourself, young Renton,' he said. 'It's against nature for things to go right. We've still got the after deck to clear and you mark my words there'll be trouble there. I feel it in my bones, man. Somebody'll fall down the hold, the beams will jam in the sockets, and all the blooming shackles'll be frozen up with rust. 'And,' he added darkly, 'I expect the cook has burnt the porridge.'

But he hadn't, and the rest of his fears and forebodings proved as groundless. The hands turned to on the after deck at nine o'clock and, going all out, got the last guy off the last derrick stowed away just as the pilot came aboard.

That wasn't the end of the pulling and hauling, however, for as the dock labourers cast off the mooring ropes, they had to be run below and coiled down snugly for the passage. By the time this was finished the *Langdale* was clear of the dock gates and headed downstream for the bar.

Cam straightened his back and, mopping the sweat off his face with his sleeve, crossed to the taffrail to stand beside Calamity Calshot and watch the jagged skyline of the great port fade into the heat haze astern.

The day was bright and the freshening breeze blowing cool out of the north-west was just strong enough to ripple the pale green surface of the sea so that it caught the sun on the front of a million tiny waves and flung it back multiplied to a dazzling glare. Northwards the coastline stretched in low rolling sand dunes, rimmed with a line of silver turf, and far to the south the Welsh hills loomed like purple shadows on the horizon. Around the stern the sea-gulls wheeled, skimming low across the bubbling wake or zooming higher than the mast-head and all the time crying as they have always cried for sailors and always will:

'Come back! Come back!'

With a little shock Cam realized the voyage had begun, and for a moment he couldn't be sure whether he was happy or sad, for the land seemed to slip away at a terrible speed, and as he listened to the gulls a lump grew in his throat and he knew that tears were not very far from his eyes. Then, feeling his hands, hard and capable on the rail before him, the power in his arms, and the cool touch of his sweat-soaked singlet across the developing muscles of his shoulders, he turned and looked ahead. And then he understood. The sadness would pass, but it would come back over and over again and always in the end it would bring him home. But now the road lay out across the shimmering sea. It led beyond the bright horizon to strange lands and other peoples, and it held, by the way, work and hazards to test and develop his body; problems and difficulties to bring new knowledge and power to his mind.

He was still standing there trying to sort out these thoughts when Rusty, released from his job on the fore-deck, came aft to find him.

'Well, Moonstruck!' he said.

Cam jumped. 'Oh, hallo Rusty. How goes it?'

'That's what I came to ask you.'

'What do you mean?'

'The mate. What did he say about the watches?'

A look of comical dismay passed over Cam's lean face. 'Gosh! I'd forgotten all about it!'

He hurried away, but inside fifteen minutes he was back, and even before he spoke Rusty knew from the dejected droop of his shoulders that the interview had been unsuccessful.

'Well?' he demanded for the second time.

Cam made a hopeless little gesture with his hands. 'No go. I tried to reason with him but he just wouldn't listen. He flew off the handle, called me a Philadelphia lawyer, and gave me a lecture on discipline.'

'And all that amounts to what?'

'Day-work for you and me.'

Rusty's face wrinkled round the eyes and his cheeks swelled, then he exploded. 'And that means chipping rust! Crikey, how I hate that job!'

Cam swung round to stare out across the sea, and gradually his face hardened and set. 'Me too. But this isn't the finish,' he said. 'It's not right, and you can take it from me old Andy's not getting away with it this time.'

3

So the *Langdale*'s outward passage began with both apprentices on day-work, and Cam seething with resentment about it.

With the tide behind her, the ship made good time across Liverpool Bay and, logging a steady twelve knots, had dropped her pilot at Point Lynus by sundown. Another hour's run brought her to the Skerries, north-western tip of Anglesey, and from there she swung away to the south on a course that would take her down the Irish Sea, past the Scilly Isles, and across the mouth of the English Channel into the Bay of Biscay.

Coming out on deck after supper, Cam saw her already drawing away from the coast line. The dark mass of the Welsh hills had faded and showed like a faint smudge of smoke low down on the horizon and far out on the port quarter. The sun had dipped beyond the western sea rim and night hung all along the eastern sky; but the twilight remained and under it the sea stretched away endlessly and smooth as a mirror.

The second interview with the mate had shaken Cam even more than the first, and he had come from it angry and baffled. If old Andy had let him have his say, then turned him down; if he had been only half reasonable and given him the tiniest shred of an excuse for keeping them on day-work, Cam would have accepted it and been content; but he hadn't. Instead he had refused to listen at all and the things he had said in his queer husky voice had made the boy squirm.

The night was so still, the soft thud of the look-out man's

feet on the fo'c's'le head could be heard abaft the bridge; so clear, the wink of the South Stack light could be seen at the limit of its range. It showed there bright as a star, one flash every ten seconds, in the centre of the smudge that had been the hills and right on the dark edge of the sea. It was a night in a thousand and it seemed impossible that such a sea could ever change to violence or hold anything of danger for those who sailed it; or that the great arch of the sky, darkening now to a softer blue and already studded with stars, could ever fill with the black menace of storm clouds. And as he leaned on the rail and stared out across the quiet sea, Cam felt its peace steal over him and gradually he became calm again.

His anger passed, but the feeling that he was not being fairly treated remained, and he knew that in spite of his bold words to Rusty there was nothing he could do about it; for aboard the *Langdale* old Andy's word was law. That was the trouble – the mate ran the ship and the mate had taken a dislike to him.

Going below at last, he turned in and fell asleep, wondering uneasily what a voyage, starting so badly, would hold for him before it was finished.

Meanwhile, the *Langdale* drove on through the night. From the bridge just after midnight the watch picked up the triple blink of the Smalls – the light on a rock off the south-west corner of Wales – and at noon next day the Scilly Isles were abeam, the hundred-and-forty-foot granite tower of the Bishop Rock lighthouse standing out above the humped green mass of the islands.

Such weather, however, was, in the words of Calamity Calshot, 'against all nature; especially for the *Langdale*,' and it didn't last.

Before they had dropped the Scillies out of sight astern they ran into fog which kept them groping at reduced speed all the way across the Channel and well down into the Bay.

Cam had known thick weather before but never anything so solid and blinding as this. There was something frightening in the very stillness of it, and the eerie way it engulfed them. The air they breathed and moved in remained unchanged except that it became cold and clammy, but outside the ship it mysteriously thickened into white walls which seemed to press closer to the bulwarks every minute yet never quite reached them.

The engine-room telegraph clanged and in response the beat of the engines slowed; then the ear-splitting blast of the steam whistle began and went on at two-minute intervals until the weather cleared again.

And now Cam noticed a curious thing. The sea around them seemed suddenly full of ships. Each time the *Langdale* blared he heard them reply with signals that varied in pitch from the throaty rattle of a hand-worked vibrator on a small sailing craft to the high powered droning boom of the electric horn on a big motor vessel. Yet a few minutes before the fog shut down he had swept the full circle of the horizon with his eyes and there was then only one vessel in sight – a small ketch making up for the Longships under auxiliary power with her sails flapping in the calm air.

It was uncanny and nerve-racking, even for those on the bridge whose job it was to locate these sounds and feel a way past them; but much more so for the rest of the crew who could do nothing about it, and Cam, pottering about the decks with the day gang, found himself longing to be up there at the wheel or the look-out.

Many sea lanes converge in the mouth of the English Channel, and over the hundred-mile stretch of water between Land's End and Ushant the *Langdale* was cutting across the courses of scores of ships – liners from the south and west, tramps deep laden with Argentine grain or Cuban sugar,

28

tankers from the Gulf ports, and coasters from the Atlantic seaboard of France and Spain. It was a bad place to meet fog. The whistles were a help, but fog plays queer tricks with sound and sometimes they had to stop altogether until the watch had located a signal. Then, going dead slow, they would feel their way past the unseen ship and hear its siren grow fainter as it drew astern. Once the white wall pressing in on them swirled and they saw a vague dark shape swing past within a few feet of their bows. They never knew what ship it was or anything about her – just the shadowy mass of her, the sharp order of an officer on her bridge, the quick rattle of her steering engine as she altered course, then she was gone into the white emptiness again.

That was the narrowest escape and by sundown they were across the busiest part of the Channel, but the fog held all through the night and didn't clear till the following afternoon. The second mate got sights then which put her well down, south and west of Ushant, and a new course was laid to pass between the two westernmost islands of the Azores.

It was just as well they were able to fix their position when they did because the sky became overcast before nightfall, and it was a long time before they glimpsed either sun or stars again.

And now the sea had changed. Its colour, which had been pale green shot with gold like a wheatfield ripening for reaping, darkened to a grey-blue like wet slate; and in place of the little surface ripple that had made it sparkle in the sun, there came a new movement, deep and vast and ponderously slow.

It was the western ocean swell. Up from the south-west it came, heaving the sea into long ridges that rolled along without breaking the oily-smooth surface. Headed across these lines the *Langdale* pitched easily, but sometimes in the plunge dipping her bows so deep the water surged inboard through the washports in her bulwarks, flooding the well-decks which from this point almost to Barbados were never completely dry.

The swell and the heavy overcast sky were sure signs of bad weather ahead, and they ran into it on the third day out – a westerly gale that blew hard for twenty-four hours, backed to south for a while, then hauled south-west and kept them battling all the way to the Azores.

In spite of his feeling about the mate, Cam had quickly settled down and begun to be really at home in the ship. By degrees he had explored her from stem to stern and become so familiar with her lay-out he could find his way about on the blackest night without a light.

Working with the day-men he spent most of his time under the fo'c's'le head. This was a sort of command post where all the gear needed to maintain and run the ship was kept and pre-pared. It held the chain locker where the anchor cables were stowed; the paint locker where the bosun mixed huge quanti-ties of paint in various colours, stirring it up in sawn-down oil casks with the blade of an oar. Then there was the lamp locker where the spare navigation lights with their strange dioptric lenses and brightly polished tops stood in long racks, and the deck head was festooned with hurricane lamps all trimmed ready for use. And finally there was the carpenter's shop with its bench and sawing trestles, the racks of tools, and the clean sweet smell of newly sawn wood.

And when the wild seas flooding the wells made it dangerous to cross the fore-deck he found his way into the stokehold. Here he would stay awhile to watch the firemen sweating in the fierce red glow of the furnaces as they fed them with coal, or raked and sliced to keep the needles of the steam gauges quivering on the red line. Then he would wander through the narrow alley-way between the boilers into the engine-room and stare at the great cranks of the main engines whirling and flashing. Down there the noise and the movement were bewildering, but he could feel the beat and power of the ship's great heart and he marked the engine-room down in his mind for further visits.

By this time he knew all his shipmates, at least by sight. They were a mixed lot and he felt particularly drawn towards some of them – the bosun and the silent carpenter, and, in spite of his mournful ways, Calamity Calshot.

Then there was the cook – a huge fat man with round blue eyes and a soft mouth like a baby's. He wasn't bad as sea-cooks go but his real talent was for the banjo. He had a beauty, all inlaid with mother-of-pearl, which he treasured more than anything else on earth, and sometimes in the second dog-watch he would bring it out, tuck his apron in his belt, and start a strumming that would soon have all hands in the galley and singing for all they were worth.

Rusty Roberts proved to be a good shipmate, too. He was generous and good-natured; he never quarrelled; he did his share of the work; and he was always ready to swop his whacks of syrup for Cam's jam. In every way he was a pal, and if there was anything at all about him that irritated Cam it was just the fact that he was too easy-going to get really worked up about the mate, and never had any ideas of his own.

Once he was in the swing of it, Cam found that day work, if not exciting, could at least be interesting. In the main he worked with Calamity and a sailor called Taffy, but sometimes he would have a job with the carpenter or the bosun himself. They were all fine seamen and without realizing it, he was learning from them all the time – not so much the sort of knowledge that can be set down in books, but little things that mattered a lot; the knack of handling tools and how to use the strength of his fingers and arms and the weight of his body to the best advantage.

31

Also there were certain jobs which were a regular routine he shared day and day about with Rusty. One of them was polishing the brasswork on the bridge. This was always done in the forenoon watch and brought him into contact with the third mate who was young and keen and never too busy to explain things.

As for the mate himself, he never interfered and seemed to ignore the boys completely. Cam had an idea, however, that like Captain Carey, he missed nothing as he stumped around on his short thick legs. He had shed his gold-laced uniform and badge cap for a faded blue patrol jacket with tarnished buttons, and an old felt hat which he hung each watch on a peg in the wheelhouse and only wore in heavy rain. And there was something so square and solid about him, something so straight and honest in the blue eyes that gazed steadily from under his shaggy eyebrows, that Cam couldn't help being drawn to him.

But still he hankered to be in a watch and if he sometimes forgot about it during the day it would come back to him at night. Then, lying in his bunk, he would hear the bell and tramp of feet as the watches changed over; and he would remember the mate was an enemy and be filled with uneasiness and discontent again.

One night, when the voyage was a week old, and this mood was riding him, he started off on a new train of thought.

'You know, Rusty,' he said suddenly. 'I've been on the wrong tack.'

Rusty rolled into his bunk and stuck his head out over the edge. 'How do you mean?'

'About Andy. I've been trying all the time to think of some way of hitting back at him.'

'Well, that's what you want, isn't it?'

Cam lay back and stretched his arms. 'It's not what I want,' he said quietly. 'I want to be in a watch, and it seems to me,

32

if the mate won't let us, then we've got to do something to make him change his mind.'

'Fat chance!' Rusty's voice was scornful. 'For the love of Mike, Cam, talk some sense. How can we make him change his mind once he's made it up about us?'

Cam thrust out his jaw. 'There must be some way. He can't be completely pigheaded!'

'That's just what he is. Once old Andy's set, you can't shift him. Not even with dynamite you can't.'

Cam puckered his long face into a frown. 'I'm not so sure,' he said slowly. 'He's human after all and he must have a soft spot somewhere. If we could find it.' He smacked his thigh. 'That's it, Rusty. We've got to find old Andy's soft spot.'

'And then what?'

'That depends, you chump, on what it is.'

All this time the wind had continued at gale force, and the sea under the drive of it had steadily increased in height. Heading right into the teeth of it the *Langdale* battered her way south and west, pitching and labouring heavily. Her well-decks were awash all the time now and she was smothered in spray that drove as high as the top of the salt-streaked funnel. The air was full of it and there was no escaping it anywhere. Sea-boots and oilskins were the order of the day, and they mostly ate their meals standing because nothing would stay put on the table.

For the most part the seas in such a gale run true, and so long as a ship meets them dead square on the bow she'll take no harm. The troughs between the crests are wide and give her plenty of room to plunge and lift again. But now and then one comes along that is steeper and shorter, and these are the dangerous moments when a ship buries herself and hundreds of tons of water thunder down on her decks.

Late in the afternoon next day the *Langdale* met such a sea and came out of it with her fore-deck a tangle of wreckage – twisted rails torn from the fo'c's'le head and crushed ventilators, mixed up with fathom on fathom of mooring wire and rags of canvas.

These wires, unlike the manilla and hemp lines which would rot if exposed to the weather, are not stowed below decks, but wound on reels fixed to the fo'c's'le head, and in the plunge she had carried away two of them. One was snaked about the deck but the other had landed on the corner of number two hatch, where it smashed through the tarpaulins and the boards and disappeared into the hold.

When the mate stuck his hawk's beak of a nose over the bridge-dodger into the gale, he saw the hatch gaping open and the sea pouring into it every time it swept the well-deck.

It had to be covered up, and quickly; and the fore-deck was dangerous. It was a job for all hands and old Andy led them to it.

A lifeline had been rigged along the fore-deck on the first day of the storm. Clinging to this and watching their chance when she lifted, they dodged across the well into the shelter of the fo'c's'le.

The first thing was to rouse out a new tarpaulin from the bosun's locker. That was easy enough, but the real problem was to get it across the deck on to the hatch, spread it, and make it secure in the cleats in the short interval between the clearing of one sea and the breaking of the next. The tarpaulin was heavy – more than even a powerful man could lift unaided – and if the sea got under it before it had been secured it would go over the side and perhaps some of the hands with it.

Old Andy scratched his chin thoughtfully, then made up his mind. 'We've got to be nippy about this, lads,' he said. 'We'll open her out now, roll it up from the sides to the middle, and put a few rope-yarn stops on it. Then we'll all get under it and when I give the word we'll make a dash for it, drop her in the middle of the hatch, snap the stops, roll her out to the sides and into the cleats. Okay?'

Beating the stiff canvas with their fists they quickly made it up into a long roll, then hoisting it on to their shoulders waited for the word. The *Langdale* plunged again and they felt her quiver as the sea crashed down on her, then the moment she began to lift, the mate's voice, no longer husky but a boom as big as the bosun's, roared out the signal:

'Go!'

Moving as fast as they could under the awkward weight of the tarpaulin, they dashed out from the fo'c's'le in a long line, up over number one hatch, between the winches, round the foremast, and on to number two hatch. Their burden dropped with a thud, knife blades slashed at the stops, the canvas rolled out, and within sixty seconds of starting the edges of it were in the cleats and Chippy was driving home the wedges on it with great swings of his top-maul.

They had made it, but only just, for as Cam stuck in the last wedge the next sea broke.

'Look out!' croaked Calamity from the far side of the hatch.

Coolly, and in one movement it seemed, Chippy drove home the wedge, then, head down and shoulders hunched, dropped off the hatch right in the face of the sea and grabbed a ring-bolt on the deck. But Cam, looking up to see a great wall of water smashing down on him, lost his head for the first and last time in all his seafaring days, and turned to run. Almost in the same moment he saw his mistake and tried to fling himself round to face it; but it was too late. The sea crashed down on him, rolled him over, and swept him away.

Frantically struggling to free himself from the choking, savagely whirling force of the sea, Cam felt himself lifted and

35

hurled through space at what seemed a terrific rate. Then something fastened round his ankle like a vice and a moment later the water cleared and he found himself lying bruised and breathless under the starboard bulwarks.

Sprawled on the deck between him and the hatch was old Andy, and one of his great hands gripped his ankle. The other was clamped on the lifeline.

They scrambled to their feet and dashed for the bridge-deck ladder just as the next sea broke, and there old Andy turned to Cam with an anxious look in his eyes.

'You all right, son?' he demanded huskily.

Cam gulped. 'Yes, sir.'

The mate's face went cold and hard again, and without another word he turned on his heel and stumped up the ladder to the bridge.

4

THE fierce squall during which the *Langdale*'s number two hatch was stove, seemed to be the peak of the storm, and by daybreak next morning the weather had eased considerably. The main body of the wind was still strong but the squalls were shorter, wider spaced, and less wild. The sea, too, though it ran as high as ever, seemed to have lost some of its smashing force and the ship began to make better time.

Thanks to old Andy's quick thinking and fearless action Cam came out of the incident on the fore-deck with nothing more serious than a few bruises. These were soon gone and forgotten, but the affair had other effects on him that were deeper and long lasting.

First there was the fact that when he was caught by the sea, he had turned away from it instead of facing it; and second the knowledge that beyond any shadow of doubt old Andy had saved his life.

Sailormen don't usually make a fuss about such things. Of course he had to put up with a lot of teasing from the deck crowd and even the cook, but he took it well and after a while they let the matter drop. All except Calamity Calshot, who had taken a great fancy to Cam the very first day out and lectured him about it like a Dutch uncle.

'You can take it from me, young Renton,' he said, 'you were a goner; as soon as I saw you turn your back to that sea, I said to myself, he's a goner; fish-bait sure as shooting.'

He had seen it all from the head of the bridge-deck ladder where he had leapt after shouting his warning to Chippy and

Cam. He had seen the curling front of the sea take Cam from behind, bowl him over, and crash down on him. The ship was lying far over to starboard at that moment, and as the sea swept him away there was nothing to stop him going over the side – only the mate.

He was on the ladder below Calamity, who saw him swing round and spring, with a single thrust of his powerful legs, twelve feet through the smother of spray. He landed flat on the face of the sea, spread out like a great frog, and one of his hands was round the lifeline, the other on Cam's ankle.

'I wouldn't have believed it possible,' Calamity went on. 'It's against nature for a man of his age and build to move so fast. But there it was. And you know those mitts of Andy's. All the seas that ever ran couldn't break that grip once it clamped down.'

Cam gingerly felt his ankle and looked past the old sailor to where a big sea curled just beyond the rail. 'I reckon I was lucky all right,' he said quietly.

Calamity took out his pipe and spat into the scuppers. 'Lucky! I reckon you were a darned fool. It beats me why you did it. Turning your back on a sea like that! It's the sort of thing a farmer might do, but not a sailorman.'

And at this Cam flushed slowly under his tan, for above all else he wanted to be a sailorman and he had begun to think he might at last call himself one. Now he realized how much he still had to learn of the ways of the sea. It wasn't only book-learning or even the training of one's hands to be skilful and strong. A fellow could have all these things and still not be a sailorman. It was to be able to meet the unexpected and terrifying, coolly and unafraid; to be able to decide what to do in the face of it and act on that decision all in the blink of an eyelid.

He saw now that not all the *Langdale*'s crew had this

quality, but it was plain in some of them – Andy, Chippy, the bosun, even Calamity and Bandy Bascombe. It was always to one of these the others looked when something broke loose and things looked sticky. How did they get it? That was the question, and he quietly set about finding the answer by studying these men and noting in what ways they were different from the rest.

That took a long time, but gradually little things sorted themselves out and fastened in his mind. He saw, for instance, that they seemed to watch both sky and sea continuously – the shape and colour and movement of the clouds; the run of the sea and how the crests curled. They seemed to smell the air and if a lone bird hove in sight, they'd pick it up when it was no more than a speck and watch it till it disappeared, and everything about it would be important to them – the direction of its flight, the way it flew, its height above the water, and so on. Then they were different in their attitude towards the ship. To them she was more than a mass of steel and wood; she had moods and feelings which they understood and to which they fitted their own.

Putting all these things together, Cam began to see they added up to something: but just what it was he couldn't quite make out, and between his watching and thinking about what he saw, he was unusually quiet and subdued.

And there was the mate.

Cam was, in his own way, as good-natured and easy-going as Rusty. At least he hated to be at odds with anybody, and the fact that he had fallen foul of old Andy had worried him all the passage. Even when he talked of getting back at him and puzzled his brains to find a way, he was hankering all the time for something to happen that would wipe the slate clean and let them make a fresh start. It seemed to him at first that the accident on the fore-deck had done just that, and all his resentment was suddenly swept away in a rush of gratitude and honest admiration for the mate. It bubbled up inside him and had to come out.

His first impulse was to go to old Andy and try to tell him what he felt, but some instinctive understanding of the strange old man's nature warned him against this. Instead, he poured it out to Rusty, and to his amazement started the first serious quarrel between them.

That day Cam was working with the second mate on manifests and cargo stowage plans. It was a desk job and he began by thinking it was all deadly dull and boring. He didn't want to be messing about with forms like a clerk in an office, and would much rather have been out on deck chipping rust with the gang or helping the carpenter to make new hatch-boards. But soon he began to see that the forms had a meaning, and there was more to carrying a cargo than just dumping it in the holds and yanking it out again at the other end.

First there was the cargo itself. It was made up of thousands of items. It included every imaginable thing from mincing machines to motor boats. There were crates of machinery, bales of cloth, cases of boots and shoes, boxes of kippers, casks of pottery, whole motor cars ready to drive away, and scores of other things for each of the ports she was calling at, and every consignment was covered by its own bill of lading.

This is a form which gives all the information about the cargo it refers to – who it is for, who from, port of destination, weight, distinguishing marks, size, where it is stowed and so on. It is made out in duplicate and comes aboard with the particular bit of cargo belonging to it. When he is sure the stuff is safely on board, the mate signs the form, gives one copy to the skipper as a receipt, and files the other.

That takes care of the cargo coming in, but when the ship gets to the port of discharge, she can't just dump everything ashore and leave it to the various consignees to pick up their own packages. There are all manner of customs formalities and port regulations to be covered and this is where the manifest comes in.

The manifest is a list of all the cargo a ship wants to discharge at one port. Each one is made out in several copies – copies for the customs authority, for the stevedore, for the receiver, in fact for everybody with an interest in the ship and her cargo. There is a separate set for each port and they are written up from the mate's copies of the bills of lading.

Finally there is the stowage plan which shows the position of each block of cargo in the ship. It is drawn on big sheets of paper on which the outline of the ship is already printed. Each port is given a colour – red for Barbados, blue for Trinidad, green for Curaçao, and so on – and the spaces carrying cargo for that port are blocked in with this colour on the plan.

Cam was fascinated and quickly got the hang of the forms, but the plan defeated him.

'What I can't understand,' he said, when they paused for a breather after checking one great pile of bills of lading, 'is why the cargo is spread about so much. Red for Barbados. Okay. But there are bits of red in all the four holds and one big patch right down in the bottom of number two.'

The second mate grinned. He was a lean-faced Cornishman barely ten years older than Cam and tremendously keen and efficient. Cam admired him for this and liked him for the gay, carefree nature that had earned him the nickname of 'Happy' Hartland. 'So what?' he said.

'Well,' answered Cam, 'we've got four holds and each of them is divided into two by the 'tween-decks. That makes eight compartments and we've only got six ports. Why not stow all the cargo for one port in one compartment instead of scattering it about?'

41

'That would certainly simplify everything,' agreed Hartland, 'but getting the stuff in and out isn't all we've got to worry about. First of all there's the nature of the cargo and the way it stows. You can do things with a bale of cloth that would play old Harry with a cask of pottery; and while a crate of machinery will ride quite comfortably against the stokehold bulkhead, the heat there would soon ruin a box of kippers or a case of tinned milk.'

Then he went on to explain how in deciding where to put each item of cargo, its weight and size, its contents, its resistance to pressure, as well as its destination, had to be considered.

'And that's not all,' he concluded. 'When you've worked that out, there's still the question of stability and trim.'

Cam scratched his head. This cargo business was a part of the art of being a seaman he hadn't known about. 'Stability and trim?' he echoed. 'What's that?'

'Well, you know what happens as you put cargo into a ship?'

'Sure. Every ton makes her ride deeper in the water.'

Hartland nodded. 'That's right, and the way she rides is her trim. The aim is to spread the weight of the cargo between the holds so that when she sails the stern will be just a couple of inches or so deeper than the bow.'

Cam frowned. 'I get that all right, but I still don't see why you can't put all the Barbados cargo in one hold instead of spreading it about.'

'But the passage doesn't end at Barbados. We've got to go on to Trinidad, then along the Main and up the Caribbean to Curaçao, discharging cargo all the way. She must be in good trim all the time, so you've got to spread out the Barbados stuff and the Trinidad and all the rest. See what I mean?'

'Yes. I hadn't thought of that. But what's the other thing you spoke of – stability? Where does that come in?'

Again Happy Hartland grinned and turned to pick up another bunch of bills of lading. 'That, old son, is tougher. It involves maths and physics and trigonometry – all the stuff that was such a meaningless headache at school. Trim depends on the distribution of weight fore and aft; stability on the way it is piled up and down. The force of gravity is pulling at a ship all the time and she doesn't stand up in the water just because we like it that way. She's really balanced on an imaginary line called her centre of gravity – so much of her weight above it, so much below. That's all worked out by the designers before the ship begins to build.'

'But,' objected Cam, 'the designers can't know what cargo she is going to carry all the time, and if they did it's never exactly the same each voyage.'

'True enough, and that's our job, or rather the mate's. He's got to decide where each bit of cargo goes. Well, if he puts too much heavy stuff in the bottom, down comes the centre of gravity and she'll roll her guts out all the passage. On the other hand, if he puts too much heavy stuff on top – in the 'tween-decks, for instance – the centre of gravity goes up, the ship's balance is destroyed, and she flops over on her side and makes the voyage with a dangerous list.' His finger stabbed at the plan where the big red patch showed in the bottom of number two hold. 'That's a heavy steam engine for rolling roads. Barbados cargo, and we'll have to shift other stuff to get it out, but for the sake of trim and stability we had to put it there.'

They bent to the forms again, and now as Cam called out the numbers and marks he found they were more than dead figures and baffling symbols. He knew their meaning and the reason for what the second mate and he were doing, and he was no longer scornful of the desk job. He remembered also that it was on old Andy's instructions the second mate had roped him in to help, and he wondered about that. Perhaps it was the first sign of a changed attitude; it might even be proof that he'd had the mate wrong from the start.

But at midday Rusty was waiting for him in their quarters and Cam was startled to see the change in him. His eyes were gleaming, his face all puckered up, and it was plain that something had happened to jolt him out of his usual habit of taking everything as it came and bothering about none of it.

'I've got it!' he exploded.

Cam grinned. 'Got what? Yellow fever or chicken pox or just the hump?'

'No, brother. The mate. I've got an idea. I was polishing the brass on the bridge and heard him yarning about ghosts.'

Cam looked blank. 'Well?'

Rusty scrambled to his feet and his face screwed up. 'Don't you see, you chump, this is what we're looking for. His soft spot; the way we can get under his hide and work on him.'

Cam threw his cap on the peg. 'Oh, that.' His voice was flat and he stared curiously at his room-mate. 'I thought you were easy about the mate. What's happened to get you so worked up about him all of a sudden?'

Rusty scowled. 'If you want to know, he caught me using metal polish on the binnacle instead of bath-brick and colza, and he blew me up.'

Cam grinned as he stuck his hands in the wash-basin. 'Serve you right. What did he say? That you were a lazy, lily-handed cissy, and good for nothing but pushing a pen or counter-hopping?'

'Something like that. Anyhow, I'm not standing for any more of his tongue. We'll work up a scheme and drive him off his nut.'

For a moment Cam was silent, thinking, then suddenly he turned. 'Listen, Rusty. I'm not so sure I want to work on old Andy now.'

'You're not sure!' Rusty spluttered excitedly, then steadied. 'You're not going to tell me you're ratting by any chance?' he sneered.

Cam flushed uncomfortably. 'It's not that, but after all that's happened I'm sure we've got him wrong. He's not a bad old scout, really.'

'Listen, Cam, it's no good you trying to come that stuff with me. If you're scared why don't you be honest about it and say so?'

Clenching his fists and struggling hard to keep his temper, Cam tried to explain what he owed the mate, what he felt about him, and how sure he was now that he had a very good reason for whatever he did.

Rusty just refused to listen.

'Save your life, my foot,' he snorted. 'That's the sort of tripe old Calamity gives you. Don't you see, man, if he hadn't grabbed you somebody else would. And if he did do all you say, is that any reason for letting him walk all over us? You're a fine sort of shipmate to have, I must say.'

'Now look, Rusty –'

'Oh, for the love of Mike, stow it! I might have known when you came aboard and started shooting off your mouth. Talk's cheap, but when it comes to doing something, that's different.' He turned away. 'You're yellow, that's the trouble.'

Goaded by the taunt, Cam swung Rusty round to face him and at that moment the mate, making his regular weekly round of inspection, stepped into the cabin. He saw Rusty white-faced and half off his balance and Cam facing him with his fist drawn back to strike and his eyes ablaze.

'Renton,' he yelled, and Cam dropped his arm and stepped back.

For a full minute old Andy looked at the two boys in silence, then, still without saying a word, made his inspection.

As he watched the cold blue eyes glinting under their shaggy brows sweep round the cabin, Cam remembered guiltily the bunks hadn't been made that morning. Then he looked round himself and saw a whole lot of things which hadn't seemed to matter before – Rusty's oilskin trailing from the settee, a bucket of dirty water jammed between the chest of drawers and the bottom bunk, a tattered magazine on the floor behind the door, dirty soapsuds ringing the washbowl. He remembered the deck in the messroom hadn't been scrubbed since they sailed, and the table was still strewn with the unwashed breakfast dishes. It was Rusty's 'peggy' and Rusty wasn't fussy.

The inspection was quickly done – that one sweep round the cabin, a swift glance into the messroom – and old Andy turned to Cam.

'Renton,' he said, and his voice, back now to its normal husky whisper, cut Cam like a whip. 'We are prepared to put up with a lot at sea, but slovenliness and a quarrelsome nature cannot be borne. They show weakness of character. This place is more like a pigsty than a seaman's quarters. Get it cleaned up this afternoon and in future see it is kept clean. I hold you responsible for it.'

Then, as suddenly as he came, and before Cam could shape the words that were bubbling in his throat, the mate was gone.

For perhaps two minutes Cam stood, his face white and jaw hard-set and rebellion blazing in his eyes, then suddenly he swallowed hard and swung round on his room-mate.

'All right, Rusty,' he said savagely. 'I'm with you all the way. Give me the dope and let's get cracking.'

5

THE *Langdale* was running a long way behind schedule. As she battered her way south and west, the long succession of strong head winds and heavy seas hammered her average down to a bare five knots, and it wasn't till the evening of the tenth day out from Liverpool she raised the Azores.

The same day gave them the first real sign of better weather ahead.

It came as a rift in the western sky late in the afternoon – a long slit in the grey pall of cloud, low down and stretching through ninety degrees of the compass from south-west to north-west. The gap was full of flame and the last rays of the setting sun spilled through it to flood the path of the ship in golden light.

The rift widened and soon the horizon below it was clear – hard and straight as a line drawn with a ruler. The sun, enormous and blood-red, hung on the ledge, then suddenly dipped, the flame went out, and where it had been they saw the hump of San Miguel Island, black against the pale green of infinite space.

It was dark when they passed it and though they were close in they saw no more than the vast shadow of it, the scattering of lights glinting along the shore, and the beam from the light-house on the point wheeling high above their heads.

Then it seemed as if San Miguel had been the gateway to another world. There was no wind in the lee of the island, and as they came out into the open again, they saw the gale had died and the sky was clear from sea's rim to zenith. The sound of the engines became loud in the hush; and, as she began to get into her stride, the beat of them picked up and became like the throb of a mighty heart.

Next morning the sun leapt from the edge of a smooth sea into a cloudless sky, and that was the beginning of a long tale of glorious days.

And now the whole atmosphere of the ship was changed. Bedding was dragged out and strewn across the hatches to air; sweaters and shirts, sodden with sea water, were rinsed out and hung in the sun to dry; and cabins were scrubbed and scoured till the musty smell of mildew was gone and they were sweet and clean again. These were the outward signs, but apart from this, everybody perked up and the nightly gathering of the deck crew shifted from the galley to the cross bunker hatch, and extended itself till four bells – ten o'clock.

Cam was affected by the change as much as any one. In a way he had enjoyed the struggle south to the Azores. It had been exciting to feel himself part of it; to stand on the deck and watch the sea, feeling its power and vastness; to measure against it the smallness of the ship and those who ran her under the black menace of the sky. Then to see her fight and win through and to know that in a way he was helping her to do it. He had got very close to the old *Langdale* in those first days and come to understand men like Chippy and old Calamity more clearly – why they sailed and would go on sailing all their lives. But he too was glad to see the sun and feel its warmth; glad to be able to eat and sleep and walk the deck in comfort again; and, above all else, glad to be able to settle down to some serious thinking, and work out where he stood in regard to the mate.

It was against the boy's nature to waver either in what he did or what he thought about people, but old Andy had him rattled. There was no doubt at all he owed his life to the mate,

48

and beyond that fact was the deep-rooted feeling that Andy was fine, not only as a sailor but also as a man.

On the other hand, it was plain he had little use for apprentices. He considered them a nuisance. He had shown that all along. And he had still less use for Cam. Why else should he have bawled him out about the state of the half-deck? There was no denying the place was in a mess, but what could he expect after a week of heavy weather? And even if the weather didn't excuse it, the quarters belonged as much to Rusty as to him.

It was neither reasonable nor fair, and his words, cutting into Cam like a whiplash, had hurt more than he cared to admit. It seemed to him then there could only be one explanation. For some reason old Andy had taken a special dislike to him. He had his knife into him and was taking every chance that came to twist it.

Slovenliness and a quarrelsome nature – that accusation was so unjust and it had been the last straw.

'All right,' he thought, 'if that's how he wants it, he shall have it.' And on the impulse he had turned towards Rusty.

Now, in a quieter mood, he argued the whole thing out again in his mind, taking it from every angle he could think of, and coming each time to the same conclusion. He had to accept it. The mate was against them both but particularly himself, and something must be done about it.

Rusty had said talk was cheap, and Cam knew now in his own mind that when he had cracked about hitting back at the mate he had just been talking. There was nothing behind his words – no plan, not even the germ of an idea out of which a plan might grow. Nevertheless, now he had decided where he stood, it was clear there was nothing else for it. To submit without a kick was unthinkable. They could, of course, apply to be transferred to another ship, but it might be two years before that could happen. Meanwhile they must hit back when and where the chance came to do so.

But although Rusty claimed to have found a way it didn't get them much further. The idea was simple enough. Somehow they must make old Andy think the ship was haunted. But how? Where did they begin? Far into the night the two boys argued these questions. Scheme after scheme was put up but not one that would at the same time be practical and prove effective.

Meanwhile the work went on, and when the manifests and cargo plans were all completed, Cam found himself with the day gang about the decks – this time chipping rust.

In a steel-built ship rust is the mate's biggest and most constant worry. Deck and shell plates, beams and frames, breed rust like a plague, and because it eats into the metal and weakens the whole fabric of the ship it is a very serious thing. Unfortunately it can't be stopped, but it can be checked, and a whole lot of any deck crew's time is spent in doing this.

The general idea is to prevent the air and moisture getting at the steel and every mate has his own pet way of doing this. On the ship side and the bulkheads of the superstructure it is fairly simple. The plates are usually oiled or varnished, then given a coat of red lead, and finished off with two or three coats of ordinary paint. But the decks are a problem. Old Andy swore by a foul mixture of black varnish, fish oil, and Stockholm tar, and the *Langdale*'s decks were in good shape.

However, whatever the mate might use, before it can be slapped on, the existing rust and dirt must be removed and the surface scraped clean. This was the job the day gang turned to as soon as the weather had fined away.

It was dull, monotonous work. Hour after hour they squatted on their heels on the deck and chip-chip-chipped away, and though they wore goggles to protect their eyes, the flakes of rust, razor-sharp sometimes, flying up from the wedge-shaped heads of their hammers, stung their faces, and worked in under their clothes, making everything very uncomfortable. On top of this there was the never-ending noise of the hammers.

Cam could have endured these things without complaint, but the slowness of the job got him down. He liked to be moving about, to be using all his limbs, not just his wrists and fore-arms. He felt as if he were chained to the plate he was chipping and he wanted to fling away the hammer and rush on to the fo'c's'le head where he could see the wide horizon and feel free.

'Gosh!' he said to Taffy as they picked up their hammers again after the midday meal break. 'I hate this job. Stuck in one place all day belting away at the same old plate. Beats me how you stick it.'

The little Welshman ran his fingers through his wiry black hair. 'Well, look you, Cam,' he said, 'it's only my body it ties down.'

'Only your body?'

'Yes, man. There's nothing to the job that needs much think-ing about, so I can think about other things while I'm doing it. My mind is free, and when I am chipping it has a fine time to itself roaming about. It goes back home and wanders up the valleys. It sees things that are grand and hears them too. It is not a thing that comes to you itself. You must reach out for it, but when you have found the knack of it the nasty jobs that must be done don't matter any more.'

All this sounded too simple to Cam, but when he came to consider it, he found that instead of letting his mind rove free, all his thoughts had been revolving round the chipping – how boring it was, how slow the progress they made, how end-less the task, and so on. Now, as Taffy had suggested, he reached out with his mind, and before long was chipping away as calm and untroubled as the Welshman.

In the course of the afternoon Cam let his mind wander round a whole lot of things, but always it came back to the problem of the mate. He raked up out of his memory all the ghost stories he had ever read and all the tales of haunting he had ever heard, hoping one of them would give him an idea, but always the background of them was a wood, or a moor, or a rambling old house. Such places were easy to haunt, but the bare decks and tiny cabins of a ship were a different proposition.

And though he felt he was just on the edge of discovering what he was seeking, he was still racking his brains when knocking-off time came. It was there in his memory – a single word that would be the key – and he kept on grimly digging for it though his head was aching with the effort.

Then half-way through supper he got it.

'Poltergeist!' he yelled, jumping up as if he had been stung.

Rusty set down his cup. 'What's that, some sort of sausage?'

'No, you chump. It's a spook.'

'Never heard of him. Where did he walk?'

'He didn't.' Cam sat down and took a pull at himself, then leaned forward and went on. 'That's where we've been going wrong. We've been thinking of spooks as things folks see.'

Rusty sat back. 'Well, aren't they? White figures gliding through trees, phantom horsemen, and knights with their nuts under their arms.'

'They're all out of date now, and if they weren't they wouldn't be much use on board ship. If old Andy saw a white figure gliding across the fore-deck he'd probably drop the hand-lead on its napper just to make sure, before he let himself be scared. A poltergeist is a modern spook. It is unseen.'

Rusty snorted. 'Fat lot of use that is. If he can't see it, how's he going to be scared of it?'

'Use your loaf, man. Andy does other things beside seeing. He can hear and feel and smell and taste.'

'Well, so what?'

'That's where the poltergeist comes in. I remember reading about it somewhere. It's supposed to be a mischievous spirit that plagues people. It makes things fly through the air, it keeps them awake at night by all sorts of noises. It gets at them in every way but it is never seen.'

Rusty scratched his head. 'It sounds all right, but does old Andy knows about them? Maybe it's only the other kind of spook he believes in.'

Cam pushed back his plate. 'That's just it. Even if he doesn't believe in spooks at all, we can get him going on this.'

'If we can fake a polter-what's-it?'

Cam set his jaw and looked grim. 'We've got to,' he said shortly, as he stood up and began to stow away the supper things.

And as if the word poltergeist had been a key that unlocked his mind, the scheme came to him simply enough in the end.

After supper they wandered along the deck to sit on the cross-bunker hatch, and one by one the crew drifted along to join them. Presently there was quite a little crowd there – Bandy and Taffy, the bosun and Chippy, old Calamity and a sailor out of the second mate's watch called Jake Jackson. For a while they swopped yarns about ships they had sailed in, then the cook appeared with his banjo under his arm and his apron tucked into his belt.

A sing-song aboard the *Langdale* was never planned. That was the great thing about them. The crowd just stuck around, some lying stretched out on the hatch watching the stars, some sitting with their chins on their knees staring out across the sea, and the talk between them would ebb and flow, some-times becoming a hot argument in which everybody joined and then again dying away. And all the while the cook would be plucking at the strings of the banjo, starting all sorts of little tunes and leaving them unfinished. But every now and then he would happen on one that awoke memories. Then some-body would pick it up and for a while the talk would stop. And maybe if there was a chorus the others would join in.

The night was warm and still, the sea smooth, and the ship was pounding along with just a slight lazy roll. The moon had not risen yet and the sky was a high arch of blue-black velvet powdered with far-off stars. Lying on the hatch, Cam grew drowsy with the peace of it all and let the sound of the voices and the music lap over him.

He heard one song finish. The banjo strummed idly for a few minutes, then picked up the rhythm of another. It was one he knew – the famous old sea shanty *Shenandoah*, and he had just recognized it when Calamity's voice croaked out:

'That's old Andy's favourite. It gets him thinking of the good old days.'

'Okay,' answered the cook, 'let her rip then!'

Cam knit his brows in a thoughtful frown. 'So,' he said to himself, 'old Andy likes *Shenandoah*. That might be useful.' Then, looking up, he saw the vast curve of the 'tween-deck ventilator against the sky, and suddenly he had it.

A little while longer he lay considering the details, then he grabbed Rusty and hustled him off into the half-deck.

'Listen, Rusty,' he said. 'That poltergeist starts doing his stuff tomorrow morning and unless you can guarantee to be awake at four o'clock we've got to sleep in spells tonight.'

'But why? What's the game?'

Cam explained. 'We're going into the 'tween-deck bunker and one of us is going to climb up inside the ventilator. It

54

stands above the upper bridge and the mouth of it is within three feet of the rail. From there we'll be able to serenade old Andy with *Shenandoah*.'

'But why four o'clock in the morning?'

'Because that's the only time we can do it. We've got to start it while he's on watch, and we must do it in the dark.'

Rusty scratched his head. His anger at the blowing up he had got from the mate had quickly cooled, and, rapidly slipping back into his usual placid habit of mind, he wasn't at all enthusiastic at the prospect of getting out of his bunk so early. 'What's wrong with the four to eight in the evening?' he demanded. 'It's dark then, isn't it?'

'Yes, but don't you see, there's too many people about then. We don't know what old Andy will do. He's quite likely to start a spook hunt, but if we make it in the morning watch we'll have time to get clear before he can get a search party raked up.'

That was reasonable enough, but Rusty continued to raise objections. The moon would be up; they would have to pass through the bunkers and might run into the trimmer; the bottom of the ventilator might be blocked with coal, and if it wasn't how would they climb up the shaft? Perhaps there was no ladder inside it. And so on, till ten o'clock.

Then Cam cut the argument short. He had made up his mind and he was going through with it whatever the difficulties.

'Look, Rusty,' he said, as the sound of four bells came to them faintly from the bridge. 'I know it means taking all kinds of chances, but if we wait for a foolproof scheme we'll still be talking about it when we get back to Liverpool. Are you standing in with me? If not, then I'll have a stab at it on my own.'

At this direct challenge Rusty caved in. 'Oh, all right!' he said. 'It's a lousy idea but I'll stand in with you.'

55

So it was agreed, and with six hours to wait before they went into action, they split the time into two watches and tossed for choice. Cam won and elected to sleep till one o'clock.

Leaving Rusty sprawled on the settee with his long nose stuck in a thriller, he turned in and, covering his head with the bedclothes to keep out the light, tried to sleep.

6

WHEN Cam turned in, leaving Rusty to stand by, he expected to fall asleep the moment his head touched the pillow, for at last the uncertainty which had worried him all the way from Liverpool was hardening into action. Nevertheless sleep was a long time coming to him.

For one thing he was excited and his muscles and senses were already tensing to meet the unknown hazards of the plan; and though he had gone over it time and time again, both in the argument with Rusty and in his own thoughts, he found his mind still prodding and probing at the scheme, trying to find new snags and ways to overcome them.

Then he was uneasy about Rusty too. He knew it was going to be much more difficult to keep awake from one till four than from ten till one, and had chosen this part of the standby for himself. But still he mistrusted his room-mate's lack of enthusiasm, and had little faith in his determination to keep awake.

And finally there was old Andy and the nagging doubts he had created by his actions. First his flat refusal to listen to Cam in Liverpool; then his orders that they should go on day work. Next his courage and drive in saving Cam from the sea; and last his apparent disregard for all right and justice in blaming him for the state of their quarters.

Where did he really stand with the mate? Was he right in thinking the fierce old man had his knife into him? And if so, was he doing the right thing about it? Wasn't this stunt he had started a waste of time? Even if it came off, and they succeeded in persuading Andy the ship was haunted, what good would it do? Wouldn't it be better to accept him for what he was and make the best of a bad job?

These questions crowded in on his mind, and though he tried desperately to push them away and in the end did so, he could neither answer them nor kill the doubts that rose from them.

He dropped off at last, however, and then it seemed he had no sooner closed his eyes than Rusty was shaking him awake again. But he levered himself out on to the deck and stuck his head into a bucket of cold water to complete the process of waking. Before he had finished drying himself Rusty had rolled in and was snoring away steadily.

Cam grinned, then, knowing his only hope of keeping awake for the next three hours was to become interested in something, crossed to the bookshelf. He ran his finger along the backs of the volumes until he came to the Nichols *Concise Guide* and the *Seamanship*. As an apprentice they were the two books that mattered most to him and he flushed at the thought that so far he hadn't opened either of them that voyage. For a moment he hesitated, then, taking down the *Seamanship*, settled into the corner of the settee. This would be a fine chance to catch up a bit.

By chance the book opened at a chapter on cargo gear and soon he was absorbed in the description of derrick rigs, tackles, purchases, and all the cunning devices a sailor uses in lifting heavy weights and awkwardly shaped bits of cargo. His face puckered with the effort of concentrating, he tried to follow the diagrams and the odd-looking formulae, and each time he came across an expression like parallelogram of forces, he remembered physics at school and wished he hadn't found it all such a bore.

But his main concern just then was to keep awake, and he

soon knew it was going to be a tougher job than he had bargained for.

He had not realized the night could be so still. There was plenty of noise, but somehow it all seemed wrapped up in a hush and it was some time before he could pick out any one sound. Then he got the beat of the engines and under it the long slow swish of the bow wave. This was the background that never changed. It lulled him, and if it hadn't been for the little unexpected sounds breaking on it at odd moments – things like the sudden clang of the bridge bell marking the hour, the heavy tread of the stand-by man going forrard to relieve the look-out, the clatter of a shovel in the stokehold – he would have been asleep in no time.

Once he did slip for a moment, but jerked himself awake again just in time and, deciding he must have something to keep his fingers as well as his mind occupied, he set down the book and took the sextant case from the chest of drawers.

'I'll clean the old ham bone up,' he whispered to himself. 'That'll keep me awake.'

He opened the brass-bound case and looked at the instrument. At first glance it seemed a very complicated bunch of reflectors, shades, and little telescopes, but though he had never used it yet, Cam had handled it often enough to know it was really quite simple. Apart from the gadgets it was a triangle of metal with a moving arm pivoted to the apex of it. The base of the triangle was curved into an arc marked off in degrees and minutes, and the bar swung across it. Then there were two reflectors – one called the horizon mirror on the triangle itself, and the other called the index mirror at the top of the arm. The horizon mirror was fixed but the index mirror moved with the arm. There were two sets of shades – one for each mirror – and they were made of orange-tinted glass, to break down the sunglare.

The sextant is the most important part of a navigating officer's equipment and Cam treasured his more than anything he had ever possessed. It is an instrument for measuring angles – the angle made by an imaginary line drawn from the sun or a known star down to the ship, then out to the horizon. The sun is caught in the index mirror, which is tilted slowly by moving the arm until the image of it is reflected in the horizon mirror, which already shows the edge of the sea. Then when the image of the sun touches the reflection of the horizon, the arm is locked by the turn of a screw behind it, and the angle read off from the arc.

That is all there is to it really. But though it doesn't sound very exciting, Cam was eager for the day when he would be 'shooting the sun' in real earnest, and as he polished away at the mirrors and the shades, he thought resentfully that but for old Andy he would have been doing it all through the voyage.

So for the moment the sextant kept him busy and when four o'clock came he was still wide awake.

As the four double strokes of the bell sounded through the night he roused Rusty, and when he had dressed himself they switched off the light and waited silently for the ship to settle down again after the bustle of watch-changing.

When the last footstep died away and he thought the deck would be clear, Cam squeezed Rusty's arm.

'I'll go first,' he whispered. 'If we're seen or heard the game's up, so walk softly and be ready to dodge.'

Although he carried a torch Cam reckoned it would be safer not to use it until they were in the bunker, and they felt their way down the alley-way in the darkness.

Then opening the door that gave on to the bridge-deck, Cam saw the first snag he had overlooked – the moon. It still hung high in the southern sky, huge and full, flooding the whole ship with a hard white light. Where they stood the house threw a narrow strip of black shadow: but the stokehold door, through which he had reckoned on gaining the bunker, was in the full blaze of it; and as if that wasn't enough, Bandy Bascombe, doing the first hour stand-by of the watch, sat smoking on the hatch within three feet of it.

Their road was blocked, but Cam didn't give up anything very easily, and in less than a minute of quick thinking he had worked out another route.

Keeping his eyes fixed on Bandy, he whispered the new direction into Rusty's ear.

'We'll have to go up over the top of the house and make it through the gratings forrard of the funnel,' he hissed. 'And for the love of Mike keep low and watch your big flat feet!'

'Okay!' whispered Rusty. 'You first. Stick your hoof out.'

With a lift from Rusty, Cam was able to clutch the edge of the deck-house. Then drawing himself up by the sheer strength of his arms he struggled on to the top and, lying flat, reached down to help his companion. As a feat of acrobatics it didn't amount to much, but they were handicapped by the fact that the slightest noise would betray them to Bandy; also they had to move quickly in case anyone came along the deck before they were under cover.

They made it safely, however, and without pausing to regain their breath darted across the top of the house into the enormous shadow of the funnel.

Here they met the second check.

The stokehold of a ship is like a vast cavern in the bottom of which the boilers are bedded. It is roofed not with plates like a deck, nor with boards like a hatch, but with gratings through which some at least of the searing heat of the place can escape. The funnel rises out of these gratings. Besides the top set there are other gratings which make landings for the long steel ladder that zigzags up from the floor of the stokehold. In the *Langdale* there were three of these – the first about fifteen feet up from the floor, the second about ten feet above that, and the third level with the bridge-deck. The door into the bunker opened off the middle one and this was what Cam was aiming for.

He knew the outside gratings were hinged in places and could be lifted like trap-doors, and his new plan was to open the section forrard of the funnel and drop through it on to the top grating. But again the moon defeated him. From where they crouched in the shadow of the funnel, he could see the squat figure of the mate in the wing of the bridge. If he should turn while they were wrestling with the grating, he couldn't fail to spot them, and there was no way at all in which they could account for their being on the fiddley at a quarter past four in the morning.

It was too big a risk to run and Rusty was for calling the whole thing off, but Cam thrust out his jaw.

'We can't get to the foreside of the funnel over the top of the gratings,' he whispered, 'but there's nothing to stop us going underneath.'

'Underneath?'

Cam was already pulling at one of the hinged sections. 'Yes. We'll go under here and swing ourselves along hand over hand until we're over the bridge-deck grating, then let go and drop on it. It's only a few feet.'

He swung his legs into the opening, and squatting on the after edge of it took a firm hold of the bar in front of him, then lowered himself down until he hung at the full length of his arms. Now he felt the full effect of the heat rising from the boilers nearly thirty feet below him. It caught him in the throat and nostrils and almost stifled him, but he set his teeth and, making his body swing gently, let go his right hand and reached forward with it to another bar about a foot ahead.

For a moment all his weight hung on his left hand but his grip was strong and sure; the swing shifted the weight to his right hand; then with his legs dangling over the vast emptiness of the fiddley he swung again, reached forward, gripped, swung a third time, and dropped lightly as a cat on the top grating.

Rusty followed. It was easier for him because Cam, leaning over the handrail, was able to steady and guide him.

Cam, feeling they had wasted enough time, immediately led the way down the ladder on to the middle grating, then hoping fervently they wouldn't run into the trimmer, took a deep breath and ducked into the dark doorway of the bunker.

And now it seemed their luck had changed. The trimmer hadn't yet started on his job of shovelling coal down the chute on to the stokehold floor and the bunker was empty except for the coal that still remained in it.

For the first time Cam switched on the torch and the roving beam of it showed they were in a compartment about nine feet high and fifteen wide. It ran fore and aft the whole length of the bridge-deck, but except for the space just round the door it was still full of coal.

Cam had reckoned on this, but he knew there would be some space between it and the deck-head and hoped they would be able to crawl or drag themselves along the top of it till they reached the ventilator. He thought the distance would be about twenty-five feet and his guess was a good one.

With Cam still in the lead they scrambled up the loose face of the coal and, squeezing themselves between the deck beams and the top of it, began to wriggle forrard.

It was tough going. Once they came to a stretch where the coal was packed tight against the beams and had to make a detour round it, and several times they were compelled to make a way for themselves by shifting big lumps back.

Then they knew it wasn't going to be easy to find the foot of the ventilator, which would be no more than a round hole in the deck-head. But though in the end they overshot it and had to spend a frantic ten minutes groping round for it, they reached it safely.

And now they got the best break of the whole expedition. Cam had reckoned climbing up the shaft of the ventilator would be the most difficult part of the scheme. He had planned to do it by standing on Rusty's shoulders to get as high as possible for a start, then 'backing up' the rest of the way – the method mountaineers use in a vertical crack; but when he eased himself into the opening and felt around, his hand came on what he knew could only be the bottom rung of a steel ladder and he almost cheered.

Twisting back, he hurriedly broke the good news to Rusty.

'It's simps!' he whispered exultantly. 'There's a ladder. You wait here and for Pete's sake don't sneeze or start banging about. I'm off.'

Less than a minute later he was at the top of the ladder staring over the lip of the ventilator across the upper bridge.

It was a little while before his eyes, strained by the long crawl through the intense darkness of the bunker, could adjust themselves to the hard white light of the moon, but when they had done so, the first thing he saw was old Andy standing within six feet of him and apparently looking straight into the mouth of the ventilator.

With his heart in his throat, Cam thought for a moment that the mate had spotted him and his instinct was to duck out of sight and scramble down the ladder. But just in time he remembered the moon was behind the ventilator, and though Andy was in the full light of it, he himself was in the shadow. Moreover, his face and hands were as black as soot after the scramble over the coal. A slight movement might betray him but so long as he stayed still he was safe.

How long he stood there Cam never knew. It seemed like hours. The backs of his legs were aching and he was terrified the coal dust, tickling his nose, would make him sneeze. But he stuck it out, and just when he felt he couldn't stand another second of it, old Andy swung round on his heel and crossed to the foreside of the bridge.

'Now!' thought Cam, and easing himself into a more comfortable position, pursed his lips and whistled the first two lines of *Shenandoah* very softly.

If Andy had heard he made no sign, and after a little pause Cam began again.

Then he knew the mate had got it. He rubbed his ear with his huge hand and looked round, and Cam could see quite plainly the puzzled look on his face. But presently he resumed his watch ahead, and giving him a minute or so to settle down Cam let it go again.

And this time old Andy went into action. Cam saw him cross to the wheelhouse in three huge strides and poke his head through the open window. Then he heard his husky voice.

'Were you whistling just now?' he demanded of the man at the wheel, who happened to be Jake Jackson.

'No, sir.'

'Did you hear it?'

'No sir.'

Eyeing Jake suspiciously, the mate jerked out his whistle and blew a single short toot that brought Bandy Bascombe pounding up the ladder.

Again the question shot out: 'Was that you whistling just now?'

Bandy looked blank. 'No, sir.'

'See anybody sculling around on the lower bridge or bridge-deck?'

'No, sir. Is there anything wrong?'

'Somebody's playing the fool. Whistling an old sea shanty. Didn't you hear it?'

Bandy shook his head. 'Not a whisper.'

'Okay. Keep your eyes open and if you see anybody about let me know.'

Then as Bandy made for the head of the ladder on the other side of the bridge Cam whistled the tune again, pitching it low in the hope that only the mate would hear it. He saw the queer old turtle-head jerk up out of the broad shoulders but didn't wait for anything else. Thinking he had done enough for one night, he dropped back down the ladder and with Rusty panting along behind him began a long painful wriggle back.

By the time they reached the open part of the bunker the trimmer was already working there and they had to lie up motionless on the edge of the coal for a full fifteen minutes before he went down below and left the way open to them. But that was the only extra difficulty they encountered, and returning step by step the way they had come they regained the shelter of the half-deck unobserved.

They were a sight – covered with coal dust from head to foot – but stripping off, they quickly got rid of the worst of the dirt; then stowing away their filthy boiler suits, dived into their bunks and dropped off immediately into a dreamless sleep.

7

THAT was the beginning of the haunting of the *Langdale*, but although the stunt had gone off without a hitch there was little stir about it among the crew the first day. Of course, both Jake and Bandy Bascombe talked, but no importance was attached to their story of the mate's queer outburst. Any one is liable to get odd fancies in the small hours of the morning, especially at sea when the moon is full; and the generally accepted idea was that Andy had nodded for a moment and dreamed.

However, when the same thing happened again the following night at exactly the same time, the ship began to hum with speculation and argument. All the famous old legends of haunted ships and 'flying Dutchman' stories were dug out and retold with new trimmings, and the whole crew was divided into two camps – those who believed in ghosts and those who didn't.

For the moment the believers were on top in all the arguments, not only in the crew's quarters, but also in the saloon and messroom. Andy, however, was not among them. He was worried and made no effort to hide the fact. But although he alone had heard the mysterious whistling, he refused to be stampeded.

Cam, cleaning the brasswork on the bridge the morning after the second disturbance, overheard him discussing the affair with Captain Carey.

'No!' he said flatly in his little husky voice. 'I didn't dream it. I heard it all right. But as for all this talk of ghosts – old wives' tales.'

'I agree with you there,' answered Captain Carey, 'but how do you account for it?'

'I can't! Not yet. But I'm going to before long.'

And Cam, watching furtively as he rubbed away at the binnacle top, saw his tough old face grow grim, and knew that in tackling the mate he was taking on the biggest job yet to come his way.

The second trip through the bunker had been very much easier than the first. For one thing, the fact that there was a ladder inside the ventilator made it unnecessary to drag Rusty along with him. That was a big gain because, though the red-haired apprentice was game enough, he didn't have the same determination as Cam; he was awkward and clumsy in his movements, and apt to start an argument at the most difficult moment. Then by setting out just before the watch changed instead of just after, he was able to cut out the perilous swing under the gratings of the fiddley.

Without that hair-raising hazard there was nothing much to it, but Cam refused to kid himself. From the first he had known he was starting a battle of wits between himself and Andy, and now he began to realize just what that meant. He must somehow keep thinking one move ahead of the mate.

His main problem was sleep, and the fact that to operate at all they had to stay awake more than half the night. Once in a while would not have mattered much, but to go on doing it night after night would be a terrific strain.

Rusty had kicked against it from the beginning.

'I don't see any sense in it,' he grumbled. 'Wasting a whole night's sleep to do something that only takes half an hour. It's crazy. Why can't we scrounge an alarm clock from somewhere and turn in as usual?'

'And if we did,' retorted Cam, 'how long do you think it would be before Andy found out and put two and two together?'

There was no way round that difficulty and Rusty's next idea was squashed just as ruthlessly.

'I know,' he popped, his face all screwed up with eagerness. 'We can start sleeping earlier. Turn in after supper and catch up that way.'

Cam shook his head. 'No. We've got to face it. Old Andy is nobody's fool and you can bet your boots he's watching everybody on board like a hawk. The minute we break any of our regular habits or do anything unusual he'll spot it and be on us like a flash. We've just got to stick it till we reach the islands. There'll be nights in then and we'll get a break.'

But on the third night there was no whistling.

Cam turned in as usual about ten o'clock, leaving Rusty to stand by and call him at one. He was asleep almost before his head touched the pillow, and the next thing he knew was the bosun shaking him awake at quarter to six.

Rusty had given up the struggle, and they had both slept through the night.

Cam was furiously angry, but there was nothing he could do about it just then for there was barely time to scramble into their clothes and swallow a mug of coffee before the bosun turned them to on their jobs for the day.

While Rusty went aft to work with the carpenter, Cam was sent forrard with Calamity to rouse out a coil of manilla and start making cargo slings.

It was an interesting job and as usual the old sailor went out of his way to teach the boy all he could. They were mostly little things he passed on, such as the rule that to avoid kinks a coil of rope should always be used from the centre and never from the outside. But they were just those things that make a sea-man and Cam stored them all away in his mind.

Calamity could see the lad was worked up about something, but behind the old sailor's long mournful face and drooping moustache a whole lot of wisdom hid and he said nothing. Instead he did his best to make Cam forget what was troubling him by talking about the sea and the islands that lay ahead.

The day had dawned clear and promised to be hot. The sky was a lighter blue than it had been, and as the sun rose higher it seemed to harden to a jade green at the horizon and filled with small white clouds moving slowly against the wind like an immense flock of sheep grazing on a hillside. The swell which had almost died away south of the Azores was picking up again and the ship pitched over it in long, lazy lurches. The sea was dark, shadowed by the rippling of the gentle south-east wind, but there was no gleam of a white-cap in all its wide expanse.

By breakfast time, thanks mainly to Calamity, Cam had himself under control again, and immediately the meal was finished he got Rusty up on the fo'c's'le head and tackled him.

'Well?' he demanded quietly.

'Well what?' countered Rusty, trying to bluster.

'You know what I mean. I want to know what happened. Did you just let me down flat or was it an accident?'

Rusty flushed, then his face screwed up. 'Oh, for Pete's sake come off it,' he exploded. 'You're talking as if you were old Andy. What's the matter anyway?'

'It matters a lot to me.' Cam knew that whatever happened he must keep his temper, and his voice shook a little with the effort. 'We started this stunt together and I trusted you. You let me down and I want to know why.'

Rusty leaned back against the frame of the windlass and looked away. 'It was an accident,' he said at last. 'I thought I

70

might as well be comfortable, so I got into my bunk with a book and I must have been asleep before I knew I was going. What can you expect? A fellow can't go on night after night without proper sleep.'

Cam dropped on to a bollard and setting his chin on his hands watched the bow wave curve away from the stempost. 'I'm not blaming you,' he said bitterly, 'but I thought if I could stand it you could. I tried to take the heavy end myself.'

'Like stink, you did. It's easy to stay awake after you've had three hours' kip.'

'Okay then. We'll swop over tonight and I'll take the first watch.'

Rusty jerked erect. 'Tonight! You don't mean to tell me you're going on with it?'

'Of course I am. Holy smoke, man, we've just started!'

Again Rusty's face puckered. 'Well, you can count me out,' he exploded. 'I know when I've had enough. I'll stand in on anything else you like to work up, but I'm not losing any more sleep. Not for you or Andy or anybody else.'

This was an unexpected blow, for although Cam had never been completely easy in his mind about his room-mate, he had helped. Nevertheless the idea of giving up just because Rusty had backed out, did not enter his head. If Rusty stood in, all the better; if not – well, he'd carry on by himself.

So on the fourth night the whistling was repeated.

During the day, Cam had given a lot of thought to the problem of keeping awake, and it suddenly occurred to him that the really important thing wasn't so much to keep awake right through the night as to be awake around about half past three in the morning. If he could train himself to cat-nap he would be able to get in a lot of sleep of a kind. The one thing to avoid was getting too comfortable. The rest was will power.

He tried it, and when Rusty had turned in, propped himself

up in the corner of the settee repeating over and over again in his mind: 'Must be awake at six bells: must be awake at six bells.'

And it worked after a fashion. He slept uneasily for several brief spells of half an hour or so, and was awake when the time came to wriggle into his boiler suit and start.

Crossing the deck unseen, he nipped down the stoke-hold ladder and into the bunker. Then just as he started up the face of the coal he remembered something and hurried back to the half-deck.

Taking his heavy overcoat and oilskin out of the wardrobe, he made them into a roll and, laying them in his bunk, drew the bedclothes up over them.

'I've got to keep one jump ahead of old Andy,' he muttered and started out again.

Fifteen minutes later he was in position and presently, when the watch had changed and the ship was quiet again, he got going.

This time Andy was waiting for it. With Bandy to help him, he searched the decks both fore and aft, then went through every cabin. The last thing he wanted to do was to rouse the ship, but he was determined to check up, and by the time he reached the apprentices' quarters he had accounted for every soul aboard, except the two boys. Softly he swung open the door, then the beam of his torch swept slowly round the room. The light rested a moment on the figure of Rusty sprawled in the bottom bunk, shifted to the huddled hump under the blankets in the top one, then snapped out:

'All right, Bandy,' he whispered. 'That's the lot.'

Again Bandy talked and the whole ship was agog by breakfast time.

'Cam,' said Rusty, as the two boys settled down for their usual spell on the fo'c's'le head. 'You're a marvel. This

72

clinches it. We've only got to keep it going a few more nights and we'll have him on the run.'

Ignoring the fact that Rusty had pulled out the previous day, Cam shook his head.

'If you think that, you don't know Andy.'

Rusty screwed up. 'But it's a cinch, man. He's proved it himself now. He heard the whistling and checked up on the whole crew. Well, what can he think in the face of that? — Either he's got the willies or he's haunted!'

'Not Andy.' Cam turned to watch a shoal of flying-fish that broke from under the bow, skim away, glinting like splinters of silver light in the morning sun. Then he swung back to Rusty. 'You say "What can he think?" I'll bet he's thinking a whole lot right now.'

'Well, so what?'

'I was lucky this morning, that's all. I guessed right. Next time I might guess wrong. But if I don't, and I go on doing the same thing over and over again, he'll get on to it in the end.'

Rusty squinted sideways at his companion. 'For Pete's sake,' he demanded, 'what's eating you this morning?'

'I've been thinking, that's all.' Cam sighed. 'You know, Rusty, you were right at the start. It's a lousy scheme and always was. I'm going to chuck it.'

Rusty sat up with a jerk. 'Who's backing out now?'

'Call it that if you like, but I've made my mind up. We were mugs ever to start such a scheme.'

'But why? It's a peach of a stunt and it's working. Now we've got the idea going that there's a polter-what's-it on his tail, we can plague the old coot's life out.'

Cam stared out across the sea. 'I know, but what good is that going to do either you or me or anybody else? Having a lark is one thing, but we aren't kids any longer and we're not getting anywhere by it.' He paused, then suddenly went off on another tack. 'You remember what you said to me the day I joined in Liverpool? About old Andy, I mean, and the crew. They'd sail with him on a raft. Well, if the bosun and Calamity and all the rest of them feel that way about him and we don't, there's something wrong somewhere and it's not with Andy.'

Rusty screwed up his face. 'You mean —'

'I mean, maybe we aren't so hot.'

The bridge bell and the bosun's whistle called them back to work just then, and there the matter rested for a while.

That night passed without incident and, next day, with a full eight hours' sleep behind him, Cam, though quiet, was more like his usual self. He was still working with Calamity on the fore-hatch, and the old sailor was glad to see him again absorbed in his job and picking things up as quickly as ever he had done.

During the night, the sky had changed again and the little flecks of high cirrus cloud had become great white cumulus which banked all along the western horizon. The blue behind them was soft, as if shrouded by a vague mist. Looking at it, Calamity sniffed the air and nodded.

'The old girl's reaching along all right now. You can see by the clouds we're coming up on the islands.'

Cam looked up. 'When will we arrive?'

'Tomorrow night, I reckon, if the weather holds. It will be good to get the old hook down and smell the land for a change.'

Cam grunted, but staring westward along their course, he felt a little spurt of excitement spring inside him and his thoughts raced on ahead of the ship.

Barbados! What would it be like when it had ceased to be merely a name and become a reality? What would it hold for him?

He knew their stay would be short — twenty-four hours at the most. But a fellow could crowd a whole lot of things into that time if he really tried, and he was determined to use every second of it. Rusty and he would be ashore as soon as they could make it, and stay till the very last possible minute, and gosh! it would be great to stretch his legs again.

'If only I could get straight about old Andy,' he whispered to himself.

Then his face lit up to a happier thought. Perhaps there, in Barbados, away from the ship for a while, he would get straight. They would be able to look back on the passage and see things more clearly; they would be able to think and talk quietly and discover at last what was wrong between themselves and the mate and what they should do to mend it.

8

THE *Langdale* arrived off Barbados just after nightfall on the nineteenth day out from Liverpool. As no cargo was worked in the port after sundown, there wasn't much point in trying to make the harbour then, and with deep water running close in under the island they couldn't anchor; but Captain Carey knew a slight but never changing current flowed to the eastward there, so he stopped the engines and let her drift through the night.

At daybreak the island was revealed. Cam saw it first as a long green hump rimmed with silver where it came out of the sea, and it didn't seem much to get excited about. But as the ship moved into the harbour the place began to take shape, and he realized it was different from anything he had ever seen or imagined.

He was working with Calamity, opening up the fore-hatches, and the old sailor named the landmarks for him as they came in sight.

'There she is, young Renton,' he said. 'Barbados, farthest east of the Windward Islands, shaped like a pear and coloured like a jewel; twenty miles long, fifteen wide, and a thousand feet high in the middle. If you follow the sea till you're twice as old as I am, you'll never see a prettier sight.'

They ran between the tiny islet on the left and a white lighthouse on the right, into a shallow bay, and anchored less than a mile off shore.

'Pelican Island,' said Calamity, 'and Needham Point Lighthouse. The anchorage is Carlisle Bay and the town Bridge-town. That's the capital.'

Then he went on to explain that the place had been a favourite haunt of the pirates and buccaneers. Hidden among the houses, which were themselves almost hidden by the trees, was a little schooner harbour where they used to take their ships when the hulls became foul with sea grass and barnacles. Here they would haul down the ship and scrape her clean again. It was called careening and to this day the inner harbour at Bridgetown is known as the Careenage.

Even before the anchor was down the first of the cargo lighters was alongside and the stevedore's men swarmed aboard. They were negroes and though some were short and some were tall they were all fine, powerful-looking men. They were full of fun – laughing and carefree – but there was a fierce pride in the way they walked and held their heads.

They took over the work of stripping the hatches and Cam crossed to the rail for another look at the island. The colour of it was unbelievably rich – first the dark blue of the deep water in the bay, changing to jade-green where it shoaled along the shore-line; then the dazzling silver of the beaches, and beyond that the green of the trees with here and there the red roofs of the houses peeping through the leaves. What were those houses like, the streets, the shops, the people? What memories did they hold of far-off days and the men who stalk through the history books like giants – Kidd and Morgan, and before them Raleigh and Drake?

Cam looked and wondered, and the excitement that had come on him when they began to reach up towards the island grew. He was impatient to get ashore and explore. 'After breakfast,' he told himself, then turned away and saw the mate standing at the break of the bridge-deck, beckoning him.

77

'Ever tallied cargo before?' he asked as Cam reached the head of the ladder.

'No, sir. Not general. Only bagged grain and cotton.'

For a moment old Andy rubbed his chin with a forefinger like a small banana, and his eyes, glinting like ice under their shaggy brows, considered the boy. Then, as if he had suddenly made up his mind, he spoke:

'All right then. You can start today. I'm putting you in charge of number two hatch.'

'Number two hatch! But –'

'I know. It's a big job. There'll be a shore tally clerk down there with you. He's responsible to the stevedore, but you'll be responsible to me. Remember we want speed but we also want every item in the manifest out and no damaged cases.'

Cam flung a despairing glance over his shoulder at the island. 'But, sir, I thought we would be –'

Again the mate cut him short. 'You'll manage all right if you keep your mind on it. Nip along to the second mate for the hatch books and get cracking.'

And with that old Andy, who had a multitude of things to see to, stalked off on his stumpy legs and there was nothing left for Cam but to do as he'd been told. Five minutes later he was watching the first sling of cargo go up out of the hold.

Andy had said it was a big job. It was also a bewildering one, and Cam was soon thanking his lucky stars for the time he had spent with the second mate on cargo plans and manifests. Those few days of mugging with figures and forms had given him a real grasp of the system and he quickly got into the swing of it.

The key was the hatch book. Making out these had been the final stage of the desk work done on the passage. They were in sets and in duplicate – one pair of books for each hatch in each set, and a complete set for every discharging port. They were made up from the manifests and listed every item of cargo in the hold for that particular port. Writing them up had been an awful grind and by the time they were finished Cam had written and checked the marks so many times he felt he knew most of them by heart. But now he began to realize how important all that work had been.

The system was simple enough. The shore tally clerk and Cam each had a copy of the hatch book, and all they had to do was to check the markings on each Barbados package and tick it off in the book as it went out. But of course there were snags. Some of the marks were not as clear as they might have been; then all the pitching and rolling during the passage had shaken things up. Packages had shifted, some of them rolling over so the marks were hidden.

It was already hot in the hold, and as the sun climbed higher and began to beat down on the decks the close air became stifling. But Cam didn't mind the heat, nor the sweat that streamed down his face and glued his shirt to his back. The ship and her cargo – the whole voyage in fact – had suddenly become real to him and important, simply because for the first time he was doing something towards it that called into action not only his muscles but his intelligence and power to make decisions. At any other time he would have been perfectly happy and contented; but the island lay only a mile away and it pulled at him all the while.

He took another look at it when Andy relieved him for breakfast at nine o'clock. It shimmered now in the heat and he could see the masts of the schooners lying inshore raking across the sky as they rolled lazily to the swell, which was otherwise unnoticeable except where it broke against the quay wall and flung up little showers of fine spray. The whole bay was full of lighters. They were small square-sterned craft, propelled by long sweeps. One after another they came alongside to be piled high with cases and bales, bundles of bedsteads, stacks of frying pans, steel pipes, girders, plating, galvanized iron sheets, three-legged iron pots, bags of flour – all the amazing variety of human needs and luxuries that made up the *Langdale*'s cargo. Then, loaded to the gunwales, they pulled slowly inshore again, the long sweeps sticking out from their sides making them look like impossibly top-heavy and clumsy water beetles.

Watching them, Cam thought how easy it would be to jump aboard the next one to leave. In half an hour he would be ashore. But there was the work and in half an hour he had to be back down the hold.

Heaving a little sigh, he put the thought of the island out of his mind and went on to the half-deck, and there was Rusty in his shore-going pants and a clean white shirt, wrestling with a stiff collar in front of the mirror.

Cam slung his cap on the peg. 'What's the bright idea?' he demanded.

Rusty turned round and grinned. 'Launch coming for the Old Man in five minutes. I'm going ashore.'

'Who said you could go?'

'Andy. Why? Aren't you coming?'

'I'm tallying cargo in number two hold.'

'Oh, blow! I was looking forward to a day out together.' Rusty jerked at his tie, then suddenly his face screwed up. 'Gosh!' he popped. 'Of all the lousy tricks! He's certainly got it in for you.'

Cam looked up. 'How do you mean?'

'Well, I ask you. Isn't it plain enough. He's never let me watch cargo, and the first port we come to where a fellow wants to go ashore and expects to go ashore, bang! and you're down the hold for the whole blinking time.'

'I hadn't thought of it like that. You think it's only a bit of spite?'

Rusty spread his hands. 'Well, ask yourself. The shore tally clerk is good enough for the after holds with the second mate keeping an eye on things. Why shouldn't the third mate do the same on the fore-deck and leave you free to go ashore? Old Andy wants to get at you, that's why.'

A couple of minutes later Rusty was gone, struggling into his jacket as he fled along the alley-way, and Cam was left to brood alone over his breakfast.

He took over the job again at half past nine and went on brooding through the whole of the day.

Work finished at six o'clock and Rusty came back aboard soon after. While he chattered away about what he had seen and done, Cam sat silent in the corner of the settee with his chin on his chest and his hands dug deep in his trousers pockets.

'Why don't you do something about it?' demanded Rusty at last.

'What can I do about it?'

'Well, I don't know. You're the bright boy with ideas. Think of something.'

Cam made an impatient gesture. 'What do you think I've been doing all day but just that? I've racked my brains till my head aches and always I get back to the same thing – Andy's the mate and what he says goes.'

'But,' spluttered Rusty, 'it's not fair.'

'Of course it isn't. And so what?'

'Well, you could kick up a stink about it.'

Cam got up and walked across the room. 'Who with? There's only the owners that can say do this or that to the mate, and if I write to the owners it will be months before they could do anything even if they wanted to.'

'There's the skipper.'

'And I'd look a nice sort of mutt running crying to the skipper because I didn't like the mate. He wouldn't half give me an earful; and even if he didn't he wouldn't interfere. That would be bad for discipline.'

'But –'

'Oh, for Pete's sake,' snapped Cam. 'Shut up, or if you must talk, talk some sense.'

Rusty screwed up. 'All right,' he popped, 'keep your shirt on. I'm just trying to be helpful. What about starting up the old polter-what's-it again? I've thought up a couple of stunts that'll put the whistling right in the shade.'

'Nothing doing!'

'But these are wowsers and they'll drive the old coot scats. We'll start by stuffing his pillow full of pepper, then collect cockroaches from the galley and –'

'No!' Cam threw himself back into his seat. 'I said I was through with that and I meant it. If you want to know, I'm sorry now we ever started it.'

'Okay,' retorted Rusty. 'It's your funeral, not mine. Anyhow, this is only the first port; maybe he'll be different when we get to Trinidad.'

'That's true, but maybe he won't,' said Cam gloomily.

And for the moment no more was said.

The cargo work began at daybreak and by noon the last package had been safely tallied out. The anchor was hove up then and they got under way for Port of Spain, Trinidad.

Cam, standing on the poop, took a last long look at Barbados as it dropped out of sight astern, then turned silently back to his work.

The weather still held fine, but the sunset that evening was the strangest Cam had ever seen. During the voyage he had learned a lot about clouds. He knew the names of the different formations and some of the things they foretold – that when the high white feathery clouds called cirrus spread over the sky, bad weather is near; and when the big fleecy ones called cumulus take on a black base and become cumulo-nimbus, there will soon be heavy squalls with thunder and lightning. But this sky baffled him.

It seemed to have three separate layers of cloud. First cumulo-nimbus – great, flat-based toppling pyramids or rough bulbous-headed columns that rose from the sea rim all round and leaned into the centre of the sky like the spokes of a wheel. Behind these were the cirro-cumulus – the tight-packed flecks of cloud which make the sky look like an ice-field. And behind that again the wisps and whorls of cirrus – like frosting on a window-pane.

As the sun went down behind the lower banks of cloud it flung immense beams of golden light across the sky between the first and second layers and reaching right across to the east. Then the light changed. For a moment it was soft and rosy, then it deepened to red; then to dark crimson that stained the sea; then the sky turned quickly to mauve, then black, and the light was gone and it was night.

The crowd gathered on the cross-bunker hatch as usual after supper and Calamity held forth on the sunset.

'It didn't look natural to me,' he croaked. 'And you can take my word, there's something brewing and it's something big.'

Bandy Bascombe took him up. 'There you go again, Calamity! You never saw a finer night.'

'That may be, but it's against nature. And this isn't any ordinary ship. It's the *Langdale*.'

'Well!' retorted Bandy, 'she's not done so badly this trip so far.'

'No? What about this thing on the mate? This thing that whistles in the night. It's bad enough being in a ship that's unlucky, but when you get into one that's haunted it's time to look out.'

'The poltergeist!' Bandy spat in the scuppers. 'He's been lying low for a while now and I reckon if ever there was one he went ashore in Barbados and missed his passage. Stop belly-aching. Come on, cooky, let's have a song – a real rollicking one to chase Calamity's blues away.'

The cook was willing and soon he was strumming away in fine style; but for once Cam's voice was missing from the choruses. He was sitting a little apart from the others, his heels tucked under him and his chin on his knees, thinking of Barbados.

The wonderful island he had looked forward so much to seeing – it was gone now and he hadn't even set foot ashore on it, just because old Andy had taken it into his head to put him on tallying.

Perhaps there was nothing more to it than that and it would be different in Port of Spain as Rusty suggested. Neverthe-less he might never come this way again, never have another chance to walk on those silver beaches and discover what lay hidden under the island's wide-spreading leafy trees. Try as he would to look forward to the rest of the voyage, this thought returned to him again and again, and each time it came he felt he had been cheated of something he could never win back.

9

THE distance from Barbados to Port of Spain is short – a bare twenty-hours run for the *Langdale* from anchorage to anchorage. It was long enough, however, for Cam to get over his black mood and build up the hope that there things would be different.

But, though there was more cargo for Trinidad than for all the other ports put together, in the end he saw no more of the place than he had done of Barbados.

The harbour was a vast lagoon. It was formed by the rectangular island lying close in against the shoulder of the mainland of South America, and the mighty Orinoco River flowed into it. Lying about six hundred miles north of the equator, and being completely landlocked with towering mountains all round it, it sweltered and steamed with heat both night and day. The *Langdale* lay four miles out from the town which looked grey and unreal in the shimmering heat-haze, and after the sparkling freshness and brilliant colour of Bridgetown, it was all a bit disappointing. Veiled with sun-haze by day and low mists at night the lagoon seemed somehow unhealthy and stagnant.

At first sight of it, with the mountains behind it, jagged black shapes in the rising sun, Cam tried hard to link it up with what he knew of its wild history; but pirates and buccaneers and frigates with towering pyramids of canvas just didn't fit into the picture, and when it became plain that Andy intended to keep him on tallying, he longed to be away.

His feeling that he was being cheated returned as the hope of a change in old Andy's attitude dwindled, and this time there came with it a rebellious anger that started deep down in him and slowly grew as the days went by.

From dawn to dark on each of the three days they spent in Port of Spain he was at work down the hold, and all the way along the wild coast of Venezuela it was the same. Their other ports of call — La Margarita, Puerto Cabello, La Guayra — like Barbados and Trinidad remained just names to him; names on a manifest or a hatch book and a huddle of buildings blazing in tropic sun, or a glimmer of lights against the dark night sky; and when they reached their last port on the Main he was ready to explode into open revolt.

Boca del Sol was the place, and it had all Barbados could claim and a lot more besides.

They came up to it as usual at daybreak and Cam was at his place by the poop winch. He saw an immense ridge of mountain, rising to six thousand feet in two strides from the edge of the sea. A sickle-shaped spur ran out from the main bulk of it at about half its height and Boca del Sol lay in the angle it made, climbing all over its lower slopes. The mountain ridge was of red rock, but recent rains had made the grass sprout all over it like a green veil.

The houses were all colour-washed — a few dazzling white in the sun but most of them yellow or pink or blue. The square tower of a church stood up from the huddle of buildings at the foot of the spur, and behind it, higher up, was a round structure of stone which Calamity said was the *plaza de toros* — the bull-ring.

Cam saw all these things in turn, but his eye passed quickly over them to the crest of the spur where a fort sprawled like a crouching animal guarding the town. Part of it was modern — the long barrack buildings inside the curtain wall, for instance – but the two bastions that hung over the harbour were mossy and weathered with age.

Calamity pointed to these bastions. 'The story goes,' he said, 'that Drake himself came here and built that part of the fort. Then he crossed the mountains to Caracas, the capital, and sacked it. They must have been real tough guys in those days, eh!'

Cam grunted. 'They didn't have cargo to watch, though.'

Catching the bitter note in the boy's voice, Calamity looked at him sharply. 'What's got into you these days, young Rentton?' he asked gruffly.

'Oh, nothing, I'm just fed up, that's all.'

'Fed up? That's queer, isn't it? I'd have thought the Spanish Main was the one place in the world you couldn't see enough of. Think of all that's happened along this coast, man; look at that queer town – the church, the bull-ring, the fort!'

Cam looked at the winch frame. 'Looking at it's just about as far as I'll get,' he said, then suddenly he was pouring out his conviction that the mate had taken a dislike to him and was keeping him tallying so he couldn't go ashore.

When he had finished, Calamity scratched his head. 'Have you asked him if you can go?' he demanded at last.

'Well, no. Not exactly. What's the use?'

Again the old sailor squinted sideways at the boy. 'Don't you think it would be a good idea to try, instead of going off half-cocked?' he said gently. 'You never know; maybe he's seen this place so many times himself and has so much on his mind it no longer means anything to him. If it's like that, the idea you're keen on going might not strike him.'

Cam flushed at the reproach in Calamity's voice. 'I hadn't thought of that,' he admitted. 'I'll ask him before breakfast.'

The *Langdale* all this time had been nosing her way in to

the jetty, and as soon as she was moored Cam ran forrard to see the mate.

He met him crossing the fore-deck.

'Excuse me, sir,' he began.

Old Andy, his mind already busy planning the work for the day, shot a sharp glance at the boy from under his bushy eyebrows. 'Ah!' he said. 'There you are, I wanted to see you. We're starting three gangs – two aft and one forrard. There's not much in number one, so we'll get that out first, then shift the gang into number two.'

'Yes, sir, but I wanted to ask you: Can I go ashore for a bit?'

The mate's head shot out. 'Well,' he said slowly, 'I shan't want you till we start number two, but I don't know what time that will be. You'd better stick around.'

'But I –'

'Yes, yes. I know. You want to stretch your legs. Well, there's no reason why you shouldn't take a dander along the jetty if you feel like it, but don't get wandering out of sight.' And before Cam could say another word, old Andy drew his head back into his huge shoulders and hurried away on his short stumpy legs.

'And that's that,' thought Cam savagely as he went along to his quarters for breakfast.

He was furiously angry and desperately disappointed, but the idea of disobeying the mate's order didn't occur to him then. When he had eaten, he mouched around the deck for a while and eventually found himself at the head of the gangway. There he hesitated, then deciding that though stooging round the jetty wasn't going to be much fun, it would be a change from the ship, he went on down the swaying ladder and stepped ashore.

The jetty was quite short – just long enough for two ships to lie alongside. He walked to the seaward end and watched the bustle going on around the ship, but all the time the piled up huddle of houses on the steep side of the mountain pulled at him, and presently he strolled back past the *Langdale* to the shoreward end.

An hour later Rusty found him there, sitting on a bollard with his head flung back staring at the fort which seemed to hang in the sky right above them.

'What ho, Cam!' he called. 'Coming up the town?'

Cam shook his head. 'Can't,' he said shortly.

Rusty, who was wearing his shore-going uniform and looked very spruce, made an impatient movement. 'Oh, come on for the love of Pete. You're not glued to the blinking ship.'

'I know, but the mate said I was to stick around. Where are you for?'

'Agent's office with some papers for the old man. Walk up that far with me. It's just round the corner.'

Cam flung a swift glance back at the ship. There was still no sign of activity round number two hatch, and even if they started opening up immediately it would be a good half hour before the derricks were rigged and the lighters alongside. The narrow, crooked street running steeply away from the end of the jetty beckoned him. How far did it go? What lay round the bend? What were the shops, the houses, like close to? There was surely time for a look at a little of it – as far as the agent's office anyhow.

He got up and dusted off the seat of his boiler suit. 'Okay, and blow the mate,' he said. 'But just round the corner.'

They set off together, leaving the level concrete of the jetty for the rough cobbles of the street.

At that moment, in spite of the rebellious mood that was on him, Cam's intention was merely to walk a few hundred yards with Rusty, then turn back. But the office was just round the corner as Rusty had said, and when the papers had been delivered, another twist in the narrow street lured them on.

'You haven't been gone more than five minutes yet,' argued Rusty. 'Let's go on a bit further. The bull-ring's just round that bend, I reckon.'

It wasn't, but there was a wide plaza with palm-trees all round it, a tessellated pavement underfoot, and a huge fountain in the middle; and by the time they had crossed it Cam had forgotten the ship and everything about her.

They walked on into a network of narrow streets.

The houses had no windows but great iron-studded doors, which were set deep in the thick walls and every one of them had a grilled peep-hole. Most of these were closed with a wooden shutter on the inside, but they came on one which was open and through it glimpsed the inner courtyard – the *patio* – of the house, with its balconies and fountains and flowering plants in hanging baskets and little tubs all over the blue-veined marble pavement.

There were few people about: a woman in black with a high comb in her hair and a shawl draped over it; a priest in a brown robe and enormous hat flat on the crown and curled up round the brim; a man riding a donkey so small that his rope-soled sandals scraped the road as it went along. The sun was already high and the heat of it beat back in their faces from the walls and narrow pavement, but fascinated by all they saw they went on, turning corner after corner and climbing all the time, until at last they came to the great dusty open space around the bull-ring.

The building itself was disappointing – just a high circular wall of weather-worn stone with narrow doors in it here and there, all securely fastened and plastered over with posters in Spanish announcing the next show – but from the foot of it the view was wonderful. Below them the roofs of the town dropped in giant steps to the sea and the jetty running out into it was like a curl of narrow white ribbon. Staring down Cam saw the *Langdale* no bigger than a toy and then he remembered the mate's order:

'Stick around. Don't get wandering!'

'Gosh!' he said. 'I'd better be getting back.'

'Aw nuts!' protested Rusty. 'You haven't been gone more than twenty minutes. The derricks aren't rigged at number two yet. Let's go on. I want to look at the fort.'

Cam turned and looked at the white road which swept round the bull-ring and climbed in great zigzags to the crest. The two old bastions Drake had built seemed to tower just above their heads. He wanted desperately to see them, to touch them and stand on them and see what those far-off fabulous heroes had seen from their walls. They were due to sail at sundown and he might never come to Boca del Sol again.

'It's not far. Only take us a few minutes and we can hare back down the hill in a straight line,' urged Rusty.

Cam stared again at the ship. He could see now the derricks at number one hatch were still working and number two was still covered up. It wouldn't take long.

'Okay,' he said recklessly. 'Let's go!'

Distances on a road zigzagging up a slope are always difficult to judge, and the crest was much farther off than either of them had reckoned. The way was steeper, too, and tough going under the blazing sun. Before they were round the second curve, Cam began to wonder if he hadn't been foolish in letting himself be persuaded. Old Andy had shown that day when he blew up about the half-decks just what it meant to fall foul of him, and his orders had been flat enough. If he didn't get back in time, there would be fireworks all right.

On the other hand, he couldn't very well turn back now. Rusty was set on getting to the top and he had agreed to go with him.

He flung a look back at the ship. 'No signs of work at number two yet,' he muttered as he pressed on. 'I guess we'll make it all right.'

They panted up the long stretch ahead of them and swung round the bend, then stopped. There, right across their path, was the first wall of the fort. It was pierced by a gateway and the great steel-shuttered gates were open, but a sentry sat propped up against the left-hand gate-post.

He was the strangest soldier Cam had ever seen. His face was hidden under a huge conical straw hat; his khaki tunic had no buttons and hung loosely over a blue-and-white striped singlet; his trousers were creased and stained and the bottoms of them stopped inches short of his dusty ankles; one of his feet was bare and the other half in, half out of a rope-soled canvas shoe. His rifle lay between his sprawled-out legs.

'Come on,' whispered Rusty. 'What are you waiting for?'

Cam frowned thoughtfully. 'Hold on a bit. Maybe we aren't allowed any further.'

'Oh, stow it, man. The place is hundreds of years old. It can't possibly be in use now.'

'What's he there for then?' Cam demanded, pointing to the sentry.

'Part of the scenery, I should think. Anyhow, he's asleep. Come on!' He started forward again and Cam followed, still protesting.

'Listen, Rusty, it's no good going around sticking your chin out. I think we'd better go back,' he whispered, catching at Rusty's arm.

Rusty's face screwed up. 'Oh, for Pete's sake!' he popped and, jerking loose, strode on.

At that moment the sleepy sentry stretched himself, and pushed his rifle out from between his legs. Rusty, lunging away from Cam, caught the muzzle on his toe and it clattered across the road.

As Rusty stooped to pick up the rifle, the soldier, wide awake now, sprang to his feet and let out a wild cry. Perhaps he wasn't very bright, or maybe he had been dreaming, and waking to see a figure in a strange uniform depriving him of his weapon, thought the fort was being attacked. Whichever it was, he was brave enough and started straight for Rusty, fumbling in his sash.

Cam saw the broad-bladed knife flash in the sun as he drew it.

'Look out!' he yelled and sprang forward.

He was just in time. Rusty swung round but was off his balance and couldn't get away, and as the soldier thrust, swift as a snake and upwards, like all knife fighters do, Cam caught his knife arm at the elbow and jerked him round. Then, knowing it was no time for arguing, he stepped in close and swung his right to the tottering soldier's jaw.

He went down, but before the boys could even begin to run, an officer in boots with another half-dozen soldiers streamed into the gateway and surrounded them.

10

CAM wasn't the sort to panic, but when he saw the soldiers strung across the road back to the town, his heart seemed to miss a beat. The whole affair had grown out of nothing, and so swiftly, it left him momentarily bewildered and breathless.

There they had been, pegging away up the zigzag road sweating in the blazing sun, thinking of nothing but getting to the top, having one quick look round, then dashing back to the ship before Cam was missed. If there had been any thought of trouble in their minds, it had centred round old Andy, and even though Cam had been uneasy at the first sight of the sentry, he hadn't attached much importance to his being there. The only thing about him that looked anything like a soldier was his rifle. It didn't seem possible he could really be on guard.

Then that careless step of Rusty's, the clatter, the cry, the flash of the knife in the sun, the blow and the sudden rush of armed figures, who now pressed menacingly close with their weapons held ready for action; and the whole picture was changed.

The boys were in a jam and Cam knew it was no use blinking the fact that it was a serious one.

Taking a pull at himself he shot a quick glance round. The sentry, holding one hand to his jaw, was edging like a crab towards his rifle which lay where Rusty had dropped it at the warning cry from Cam; the officer, his highly polished boots gleaming and his spurs jingling, wa﹘ coming in towards them from the right; three of the soldiers were behind Rusty, the remainder across the road below the gateway.

Cam looked longingly down the road. He was quick on his feet and reckoned he could easily dodge the three men in his way. If he were to run straight for them, then at the last moment pretend to swerve to the left, but instead duck and weave to the right, he could be over the edge of the road and under cover before they knew what was happening. But there was Rusty, and he was hopelessly cornered.

With a little sigh of resignation, he gave up the idea of flight almost before it was born and, licking his barked knuckles, swung round on the officer. As he saw it, all that was left was to explain exactly what had happened and to trust to the man's common sense to release them.

That seemed simple enough, but Cam had overlooked two things: first that the officer knew no English, and second that he himself, with his cap thrust back off his lean face, his jaw set pugnaciously with the strain of the moment, and his fists still clenched, looked anything but a peaceful figure.

The officer was taking no chances. He rapped out an order, and before Cam had taken two paces forward both boys were seized and roughly hustled away up the hill.

They struggled desperately but it did them no good. The soldiers were evidently well used to handling unruly prisoners and the sentry in particular was eager to get a bit of his own back.

'Lay off, Rusty,' called Cam at last. 'There's not an earthly just now. Act dumb and keep your eyes skinned for a chance to break.'

'Okay,' panted Rusty. With a twist of his sturdy body he dug a bony elbow into a soldier's ribs, then walked on between his captors as gentle as a lamb.

The little procession turned another bend in the road, then at the head of the next stretch passed through a second gate which gave entrance to a wide dusty open space they guessed was the parade ground. On the right as they came in, it was bounded by the high wall of the fort, curving away out of sight round the shoulder of the hill; to the left the hill rose sheer and, in spite of all the height they had gained, it still towered high above their heads, throwing the immense square into shadow. Numerous narrow doorways were cut into the face of the rock, and Cam guessed the whole upper part was honeycombed with galleries.

The officer gave them little time to take in their surroundings, but as he rushed them across the square, Cam instinctively gathered what detail he could of the place. He saw there were very few men about and most of them seemed to be either sitting or leaning against the walls; he noted that the door they were making for was in the rock-face far to the left of all the rest; then a moment later he was stumbling along a dimly lit passage at Rusty's heels, counting his paces.

One hundred steps they went straight between rough hewn rock walls, then the passage turned sharply to the right. Before them now on the left were a number of doors. The first was open and occupied by three men – obviously the guard-room. The rest were cells, old and crude but immensely strong.

There was a quick exchange of words between the officer and the guard, then the boys were pushed into the fourth doorway along; the door slammed shut on them and, as if to hammer home the fact that they were trapped, the great steel locking-bar dropped across it with a clank that went on echoing through the gallery long after the footsteps of the soldiers had died away.

The cell was no more than seven feet long and six wide. It was lighted by a barred opening high up in the wall opposite the door, and the only furniture in it was a wooden bench and a small earthenware water jar.

Rusty threw one despairing glance round the place then

dropped on the bench and shivered. His face seemed more screwed up than Cam had ever seen it. 'Gosh!' he popped at last. 'We're in for it now all right. What do you reckon they'll do next?'

Cam stuck his hands into his pockets and kicked the water jar. 'Search me. What's old Andy going to do when they start cargo at number two and I'm not there?'

'Old Andy? For Pete's sake forget him for a bit. If you hadn't been chewing the fat about getting back to old Andy we wouldn't have got into this jam!'

Cam swung round. 'You mean if you hadn't been so pig-headed and had watched where you put your big flat feet!' he retorted, then, seeing the strained look in the other's face, he caught at his temper and went on quietly. 'Listen, Rusty, forget it. Flying off the handle at each other isn't going to do any good. We're in a spot. Okay, never mind how we got into it or whose fault it was, what we've got to worry about is what the tallow-faced guy is cooking up for us and what we can do about it.'

Rusty dropped his chin on his hands. 'What can we do?' he demanded helplessly.

'The first thing is to try and work out just what we might expect to happen.'

'That doesn't take much thinking about. Old Andy's probably ramping around looking for you now, but when he doesn't find you he'll think you're lying low to dodge a row. The ship sails at sundown and nobody will think of checking up to see if we're aboard. She'll be at Curaçao before we're missed and she won't come back.'

'No, but the Old Man will get the consulate on the job and the agent. They'll soon locate us.'

'And then?'

'Well, then they'll get us out.'

'But when?' Jumping up, Rusty began to pace to and fro across the cell. 'You don't understand how serious this is. If the Old Man himself knew we were here and came tearing up today he could probably bluff them into letting us go and wiping the whole thing off the record, but once the ship sails and we're caught up in the cock-eyed machinery of the law we might be here for years. Don't you see, man, once the ship has gone we're anybody's business, which is the same as nobody's, and neither the agent nor the consul will lose any sleep worrying about us or any sweat trying to get that door open.'

Cam whistled through his teeth. "I hadn't thought of that,' he confessed. 'You're not pulling my leg, I suppose?'

'I wish I was. I've heard of fellows picked up just like we were who stewed in jail for years. The trouble is that once you're nobbled it takes time to start anything working to turn you loose, and all that time the charge against you is growing. I expect his nibs with the spurs is busy writing it out against us now, and I bet it's as long as my arm already.'

'That settles it then. We've got to get out of here today.'

'Out of here!' Rusty waved his hands round the bare walls of the cell.

'Why not?' Cam was brisk. He saw Rusty had taken a pretty bad scare and knew the best thing to jolt him out of it was action. 'People have escaped from such places before. Why shouldn't we?'

'But you're crazy! Look at it – the walls, the door . . .'

Dropping on to the bench, Cam began to unlace his shoes. 'We'll look at them in a minute,' he said. 'The window seems the best bet to me.'

'But the bars!' Rusty pointed up to where the beam of sunlight was split by two vertical bars.

'Listen, Rusty.' Cam threw off one shoe and stooped to the other as he talked. 'I've got an idea. Remember what this place looked like from below – a crouching animal with the two old bastions along the sides of the spur like paws. One of those bastions – the south-west one – hung right above the jetty and the ship. Right. Now remember how we crossed that square and how the gallery ran when they pushed us into it? If my reckoning's right we're in the south-west bastion.'

Rusty had stopped his pacing and now scratched his head. 'So what?'

'Well, if I'm right, that window looks right down on the jetty and we'll be able to pass a signal through it.'

'But how? We've got no flags or lamp.'

'Heliograph,' said Cam shortly. 'The sun and your wrist-watch. If we can catch somebody's eye – old Calamity's, for instance, this place fascinates him, he's always gawking up at it – then we spell out a message in morse and Mother Carey will be up here in two shakes to hook us out.' He flung down his other shoe and got to his feet. 'We'll have a dekko any-how. I'll just about reach it off your shoulders.'

Rusty, still grumbling, but unable to resist Cam's drive and determination, made a back. 'Oh, all right,' he growled, 'but I still think you're crazy.'

Cam grinned and, buckling on the watch, scrambled up on to Rusty's shoulders; then at full stretch he found he could just get a grip of the bars.

With his heart pounding he pulled himself up and, after a struggle, which left him breathless, contrived to get one arm hooked round the bars and a knee cn the edge of the opening. Then, as he pressed his face against the rust-pitted metal and stared out, his whole body seemed to go numb with the shock of disappointment.

The wall of the cell was at least six feet thick and the open-ing narrowed out towards the rock face. His reckoning had been dead true; they were in the south-west bastion, and the sun was just right for heliographing, but because of the thickness of the wall and the angle of the aperture, all he could see of the ship was the truck of the mainmast and the top half of the house-flag fluttering below it. So far as signalling to her went, the *Langdale* might as well have been on the other side of the Atlantic.

For perhaps a minute longer he clung there, staring out at the blue sea and sky, then Rusty's voice from the floor roused him.

'Any luck?'

Dropping lightly back on the floor of the cell, Cam shook his head. 'No go,' he said and explained the situation.

Rusty sat down on the bench heavily. 'That means we're sunk.'

'Not on your life,' retorted Cam. 'It means we can't count on Mother Carey, that's all. It's up to ourselves now.'

'Same thing!'

'I'm not so sure. Let's have a look around.'

'I've looked. The walls are solid rock and it would take dynamite to shift the door. The hinges must weigh a hundredweight each and they're set deep into the wall. Give it up, Cam. There isn't a hope.'

Still reluctant to admit defeat, Cam prowled round the cell, tapping at the walls, sounding the floor, and coming back again and again to the massive door; but gradually his confidence dwindled, and in the end he too gave up the struggle and joined Rusty on the bench.

They sat there a long time, not speaking, not moving – just staring moodily at the dust motes dancing in the beam of sunlight from the opening above their heads. It poured through the semi-darkness of the cell like a stream of dusty gold. The rectangle of light it spilled on the worn floor-stones seemed to fascinate them both. It was all the outside world that was left to them; it was life and warmth and folks they knew – everything that mattered; but it came to them from far off like a memory, and the barred shadows across the pool made a mockery of the hope it raised.

Then, as the sun crossed the meridian and started the long dropping swing towards the western sea rim, the pool of light began to lengthen and move slowly across the floor.

'If only we could do something!' whispered Cam at last. 'Let's talk; tell stories; sing shanties; play games – anything but sitting here waiting like this. We'll go scatty this way.'

Rusty hooked his heels on the edge of the bench and wrapped his arms round his legs. 'I've had enough fun and games to keep me going for a while,' he said. 'What I want most of all is to get out of here and if I can't have that, then I want some grub. Gosh! I'm starving. I don't suppose they'll feed us more than twice a day but I wish they'd get a move on.'

'Oh, you and your nosebag!' Cam got up and moved restlessly round the cell. Talking just for the sake of breaking the unbearable silence he went on. 'Can't you think of anything else when we're in a jam like this. Grub! Do you expect Bug-whiskers with the spurs to come in twice a day with a plate of ham and eggs for you?'

'If he came in this minute with a hunk of bread and a jug of water I'd fall on his neck!'

'You'd fall –' Cam stopped and looked at Rusty with his mouth open, then moved across to the bench and sat down as if all the strength had suddenly gone from his legs.

'What is it?' demanded Rusty. 'What's gone wrong?'

Staring with unseeing eyes over the other lad's shoulder. Cam repeated his last words slowly as if they were a key to a riddle that still eluded him. 'You'd fall on his neck –' Then suddenly he swung round. 'You've got it, Rusty. Our only chance. Don't you see, they'll have to open the door to give us grub. When they do that we'll have to nobble the sentry – fall on his neck like a ton of bricks – lock him in here and take our chance of doing a bunk.'

'But suppose they send two men?'

'Then somehow we'll have to wangle them both inside and nobble the other one too. What do you say? Are you game?'

Rusty scratched his long chin thoughtfully. 'It won't be easy,' he said slowly. 'Those guys are tough. And suppose we do get out of the cell, what then? There's still the guard-room to pass, the gallery, the guard on the entrance, and that long road back to the ship. It's a thousand to one against us making it.'

'Maybe not both of us,' admitted Cam, 'But if one can get clear and reach Ma Carey before the ship sails, that's all we want. If we plan for that from the start it will give us a big bulge. First of all they won't expect us to make a break; second, it's a hundred to one they'll be eating in the guard-room when they send the grub to us – that will give us a chance to sneak past; third, once they are on our tails they'll expect us to stick together, but we won't. Your job will be to get through and mine to hold up the hunt if it starts. Okay?'

Rusty thrust out his hand. 'Okay, I'm in with you.'

Then, with Rusty at last breaking free of his despairing mood and putting all his mind to the problem, they went into a huddle and worked out a plan step by step, while the sunlight, unheeded now, reached the edge of the floor and began to climb up the door. They went over the scheme time and time again, trying to provide for everything that could happen, altering here, tightening there, until at last it seemed as perfect as they could make it.

'Remember, whatever happens,' Cam repeated, 'don't turn

back, and for Pete's sake get off the road into the rough as soon as you clear the gate.'

Then they settled down to wait.

The shaft of sunlight moved imperceptibly but steadily higher.

Sitting there listening for the sound of footsteps outside the door, and hearing only the thump of their own hearts, it seemed to them that time had ceased to move. Fancy played them tricks. Staring at the pool of light creeping up the door, Rusty saw it begin to spin; then it widened and deepened and he felt an over-powering urge to take a header into it. Just in time he wrenched away his head and broke the spell. Cam was in no better way. He had a feeling that the cell was no longer part of the solid mountain, but an old stone coffer in which they were falling, falling, spinning through endless space, and he clung to the bench until the ache in his fingers brought him back to reality.

The sun was low now and the light seemed to move more quickly up the door – knee high, waist high, breast high, head high. Then, at last, the sound of footsteps. Silently the two boys took up their positions on either side of the doorway, and with a new thrill of hope saw the light would be full in the sentry's face as he entered.

'Only one!' whispered Cam and stuck up his thumb.

The locking-bar dropped with a thud and the door swung open. With his rifle under one arm and a dish of food in the other the sentry strode in.

He hadn't a chance. From his place flat against the door-post Cam hooked him round the throat and at the same moment Rusty reached out sure hands from behind the door and plucked his feet from the ground. They had thought of everything. Cam caught the falling rifle against his thigh and let it slide gently to the floor, while Rusty juggled the dish on to their victim's chest. Then they carried him to the bench, gagged him with their handkerchiefs, and bound him with his own sash until he looked a fair imitation of a mummy.

Leaving the rifle where it lay, and the door swinging behind them, they crept out into the passage.

Ahead of them they saw the hard square of light from the open door of the guard-room, and heard the clatter of dishes and the hum of voices. This was the dangerous stretch and they had to move quickly.

The gallery was badly lighted, and once they were past the guard-room door they would have their backs to the men inside it. Cam reckoned that their best bet was to walk on briskly, trusting that if they were seen from behind they'd be taken for people of the fort. He hoped this way to get out in the square before somebody thought to chase up the sentry and raised the alarm.

With Rusty in the lead they set off. There was no need to worry about their footsteps. The guard was making enough noise to drown the tread of a platoon. As they hurried past the door Cam squinted sideways and saw two of them were having an argument across a long deal table, and all the rest seemed to have taken sides. Then with another kind of thrill he saw the square of daylight at the end of the gallery, and resisting both the urge to run and the temptation to look back, he pressed steadily on in Rusty's wake.

A hundred paces he had counted along that stretch coming in and now he tallied them back.

Ten. Twenty. Twenty-five. Thirty.

Then the babble of voices behind them swelled into a roar; he flung a glance over his shoulder and saw the guard-room door choked with men. The sentry had been discovered.

'Pick 'em up, Rusty. They're on to us!' he yelled.

Rusty needed no urging. Throwing up his head and tucking his elbows into his ribs, he pounded towards the mouth of the gallery, Cam plugging along behind him, working out their chances as he ran.

It looked easy. They had a good thirty yards' start and Cam was just thinking of thumbing his nose to the crowd at his back when the officer who had arrested them suddenly stepped from nowhere into the entrance of the gallery.

Rusty faltered and checked but Cam didn't stop. He knew there was no time and one man was easier than six, and he had foreseen something like this and knew what had to be done. One of them must get through.

'Keep right behind me and when I go for him, swerve left,' he panted as he slipped past Rusty into the lead.

The gallery widened towards the mouth and that helped. He saw the sun glint on the man's spurs and heard the button of his holster snap as he dragged at his pistol. Then, judging his distance perfectly, Cam dived for him in a flying tackle. His arms closed round the man's legs just above the knees and they went down together with a thud that seemed to shake the fortress.

'Over the edge, Rusty!' Cam yelled, driving his head into the soft stomach under him, and for a moment he thought he heard the quick beat of his shipmate's feet. Then a gentle hand touched his shoulder.

'All right, Cam,' said a cool quiet voice. 'Don't worry the man. He isn't a bone!'

He looked up, and there, smiling down at him, was Captain Carey.

11

WHEN Cam stood up and backed cautiously away from the furious officer, he saw men running into the parade ground from every corner. Whistles were shrilling and alarm bells ringing all over the great hump of the mountain-top, and the square hummed like a hive of angry bees.

In the centre of it all, Captain Carey stood cool and unruffled.

Returning on board after completing the ship's business late in the afternoon, he had been told by the mate that the two boys were ashore. Normally he would have thought nothing of it, for he knew how easy it was to wander off in a strange place. But throughout the day he had been hearing rumours of some disturbance at the fort, and the two things had clicked in his mind. He was a man who always acted on hunches and stopping only to pick up the most influential officer he knew – the chief of customs – he had driven in a hired car straight up to the fort.

He arrived just in time to see Cam make his flying tackle and Rusty come loping like a hare out of the gallery.

He had the whole story in a couple of minutes. Then with the two boys beside him and the tubby little customs chief at his back he waited for the upheaval to settle and the commandant to appear.

He came at last, hurrying from his quarters higher up the hill, and Cam took heart at the sight of his jolly fat face and twinkling black eyes; but when the customs man had introduced Captain Carey and explained his business, he looked grave.

'There must be a full inquiry,' he said in English, and presently the boys found themselves in an office on the far side of the square. Taking his place behind an enormous desk the commandant waved the customs chief and Captain Carey to chairs on either side of him, and motioned the boys to stand on the left. Then he spoke to an orderly who brought in the lieutenant of the guard, the sentry Cam had clipped on the jaw, and the man they had trussed up in the cell.

When each man in turn had made his report and been dismissed, the boys gave their version; then the commandant leaned back in his chair and plucked at his bottom lip.

'So,' he said at last, 'The sentry was asleep, you tripped over his rifle and stooped to pick it up for him. My men tell a different story.'

'They are hardly likely to admit the truth, are they?' put in Captain Carey. 'My boys would not knowingly court trouble.'

'Your boys! The lieutenant of the guard has another name for them. Desperadoes. The tall one felled a sentry who tried to prevent him entering the fort; they overpowered the man who was guarding their cell; and threw down the officer who tried to hold up their escape. What breed of boy is it, Señor Capitán, that will attack armed men with naked hands?'

'The same breed that laid the foundations of your fortress centuries ago, Señor Comandante.'

The commandant looked up and his dark eyes gleamed. 'True, and it changes little. But what are we to do? My lieutenant has been monstrously handled. He is a proud man and hurt in his pride. He demands that we protest and claim recompense.'

Captain Carey smiled. 'By all means, Señor Comandante. But would it be wise?'

'To admit my command is so undisciplined that sentries sleep at their posts, so inefficient two beardless boys can defy all the force we can muster?' The soldier stood up and banged his fist on the desk. He had made his decision. 'No. Señor Capitán, I shall erase the affair from the records.'

Captain Carey thanked him for his courtesy and tolerance, and the boys apologized for the trouble they had caused; then, after handshakes all round, they were in the car and speeding back to the ship.

She was ready for sea – the pilot on board, moorings singled up, and the crew at stations. They hurried up the gangway on to the bridge-deck and there Captain Carey dismissed the boys.

'I want to see you both in my room at ten o'clock in the morning,' he said, and his face as he turned away towards the bridge gave them no hint of his thoughts.

They helped to stow the mooring lines and before they had finished night shut down on the Caribbean. When they went to supper, Boca del Sol was no more than a shimmer of lights on the shadow of the mountain astern.

Cam was very quiet that evening. He was worried. The day's adventure had ended happily enough but he got no satisfaction from that. They had been lucky and things might easily have gone the other way. And there was the interview with Captain Carey to face next morning. The skipper had been great – so quiet and sure; so kind and understanding. But when all was said and done he was skipper and they would be on the carpet before him in the morning. What would he say? What would he think? He was a quiet man but he seemed to know such a lot. His eyes bored into a fellow and seemed to read him like a book, and Cam wasn't at all sure he wanted Captain Carey to know all that was in his mind.

And on top of all this he was worried about the mate. Old Andy's orders had been clear. He had broken them. All the way back to the ship he had been bracing himself for the row that would follow. He had pictured the mate waiting for him at the head of the gangway, his head thrust out from his great shoulders, his eyes cold and hard as ice, his voice a husky whisper cutting like a whip; and when he wasn't there, Cam expected a call to the bridge as soon as they had cleared the port. That call didn't come and as the evening wore away he became more and more uneasy. What was the mate thinking? What would he do about the defiance of his authority?

Rusty, however, seemed untroubled. 'What are you worrying about?' he demanded. 'The skipper can't have us shot. He can only tell us off and that won't break any bones.'

'It's not only the skipper, but old Andy.'

'Well, the same thing goes for him. He can only blow you up.'

Cam frowned. 'I know, and that's okay. I reckon I've got that coming and if he'd been waiting for us and walked into me when we showed up, I wouldn't have minded. But he's done nothing. What's he thinking? What's in his mind?'

Rusty snorted. 'Oh, come off it. What's it matter? He's never been anything else but a pain in the neck to you. He's had a down on you all the voyage. Well, you've given him something to moan about now. Let him get on with it.'

But Cam couldn't help feeling that it did matter; that somehow the day in Boca del Sol had cost him more than barked knuckles and a few bruises, and he slept uneasily that night.

Rusty was still very cocky next morning, but between breakfast time and ten o'clock his bravado seemed to have oozed away and it was Cam who led the way to the skipper's cabin and rapped on the door, Rusty trailing behind looking as if he wished he were back in the fortress of Boca del Sol.

Captain Carey was sitting at his desk and his face told them nothing. Nodding to them to wait, he finished the entry he was making in the log book, then swung round in his chair.

'Now,' he said quietly. 'What have you to say for yourselves? You're longest in the ship, Rusty. You start.'

Rusty flushed and shuffled his feet. 'Well sir, there's not much to tell. I had some papers to take to the agent's office. The second mate gave them to me and said I needn't hurry back. Renton went with me and we walked on up the town. Then we thought we'd go on to the top of the ridge and back. We didn't know the fort was used. We thought it was a ruin. And I was only picking up the sentry's rifle for him. We'd have come back then but he went for me with a knife, and before we knew what was happening a whole crowd grabbed us and ran us in.'

'And that's all?'

'Yessir.'

'How about you, Cam?'

Cam jerked up his head and looked into Captain Carey's face. 'There's nothing I can say, sir. The mate told me not to leave the jetty and I did. I – I'm sorry, but that doesn't seem much use now.'

For a whole minute Captain Carey looked from one to the other of the boys in silence, then he leaned towards them. 'Now look, boys. What happened yesterday might have been serious, but we were lucky and it came out all right in the end. Now I'm not going to blow you up about it. I believe you're a couple of sensible lads. You've had your lesson and you won't get into a jam like that again.'

'You bet we won't, sir,' said Cam earnestly and Rusty mumbled.

'Right then. I'm going to forget it ever happened. That's all. You'd better get along to your work now.'

Rusty's face screwed up. 'Thank you, sir,' he popped, and dragging open the door he was out on deck before the skipper could say another word.

Cam hesitated a little, opened his mouth as if he wanted to say something, then slowly followed his room-mate.

Captain Carey watched him in silence till he was over the door coaming, then as if suddenly making up his mind, called him back.

'Sit down, Cam,' he said gently, pointing to the corner of the settee opposite his chair. 'I think it's time you and I got things straight. What's gone wrong?'

Cam spun his cap between his knees. 'Nothing, sir. That is, I – I'm sorry about yesterday, as I said.'

'I can see that quite plainly, but there's more to it than that. A fellow like you doesn't go flying off the handle for nothing. There's some trouble between you and the mate, isn't there?'

Cam was silent.

'Now look, son,' Captain Carey went on. 'I don't want you to think I'm poking my nose into your affairs, and I certainly don't want you to tell me anything you'd rather not, but the master of a ship sees a whole lot that's hidden from other people on board and I've seen things this voyage and what I haven't seen I can guess.' He paused, then leaned forward and tapped the boy on the knee. 'A ship is a queer set-up, you know, Cam. Thirty-eight men, all kinds, thrown together for months on end. They've got to fit into each other and pull together. We never know when we'll have to buck against wind or sea or fog or any of the hazards that might come our way, and we can't do that if we are bucking against each other. Can we?'

Cam looked down at his hands. 'No, sir.'

'Well then, I'm asking you what you've got against the mate. I'm asking not so I can hold it against you or drive you into a corner with it, but so I can help you put things straight, and what you tell me will go no further.'

Cam frowned and again his face flushed. 'Perhaps it would be easier if you asked the mate what he's got against me, sir.'

'You think he has something on you?'

'I know he has. I'm sure of it.'

'Why?'

'If he hasn't, why did he keep me on day work all the outward passage instead of putting me in a watch? And why did he keep me tallying cargo at Barbados and Trinidad and all along the Main so I didn't have a chance to go ashore; then when I asked him yesterday, why did he say I wasn't to leave the jetty?'

Captain Carey drummed his fingers on the desk, and for a while he looked at Cam thoughtfully. 'So,' he said at last, 'you feel he's been giving you a raw deal, but tell me, Cam, what work did you do on the passage out?'

'I did some chipping. A bit of painting. I worked with the carpenter making hatch-boards and with Calshot on cargo gear, and I was a long time with the second mate on the manifests and stowage plans.'

'You didn't like those jobs?'

'Well, sir –' Cam hesitated. 'It wasn't that. It was all interesting – even the chipping, once I got Calamity on talking about rust. But I'm an apprentice, sir. One day I hope I'll be a mate in charge of a watch and I want to learn how to do it now – not waste my time with things that don't matter.'

The skipper smiled. 'But surely you have seen there is more to being a ship's officer than driving a ship between ports.'

'Yes, sir. I see that now. There's the cargo work and the maintenance.'

'There's more than that, Cam. There's being able to make decisions and carry them through; there's being able to keep your head when things bust loose; there's being able to hold the ship together with odds and ends when she gets smashed up. And, most of all, there's being able to hold your crew behind you as a crew, and keep them fighting and believing in you when hunger and cold and the savagery of the sea has left them with nothing to hang on to but that belief. It's a big job – a man's job.'

He went on and Cam, as he listened, began to understand for the first time just how much there was in this business of being a ship's officer. He saw how every little niggling thing old Andy had given him to do counted – how one developed his muscle, another his eye, a third his judgment of time and distance; how each hour he spent working with the foremast hands taught him to know and understand them better against the day when such men as they were would look to him for guidance. And gradually it came clear to him that every job the mate had given him had been carefully chosen to help him on his way to the bridge.

Captain Carey finished at last. 'So there it is,' he said. 'You can put in your time, swot up navigation at a cramming school, get the rule of the road and enough stock answers to stock questions on seamanship out of any decent book on the subject, and get by. You'll have a nice certificate with gold lettering on the cover, but you won't be a seaman and you'll never know when something's going to break that you aren't big enough to handle. That's one way, but it isn't mine or old Andy's. He believes, as I do, that you must know what a ship looks like from the deck as well as from the bridge; you've got to know the feel of a wire or a rope in your hands as well as the weight it will carry from the formula in the book. See what I mean?'

Cam nodded dumbly.

'That's looking at it from your side. Two ways of tackling a job of serving your time. Well, looking at it from the mate's side there are two ways as well. As an apprentice you are his responsibility. Now a mate carries a lot of responsibilities and if he made any one of them as light as possible, nobody could blame him. It would be easy to stick the apprentices in a watch and forget about them; let them decide for themselves what they should learn or even if they should learn at all or just put in their time any old how. That's not old Andy's way. He's a queer chap but a fine seaman. He might growl at you now and then but he takes his responsibility towards you very seriously.'

'Then you think all the time he was trying to help me forward, sir?'

'I don't think it. I know it.' Again Captain Carey looked steadily and thoughtfully at Cam for a moment, then he went on. 'You're wondering where you stand with him now – after yesterday? And why he hasn't sent for you and told you off about it?'

'I'm thinking I've made an awful muck of things, sir.'

'So you have. You see it didn't matter a great deal to him if you stayed on the jetty or not. I mean it didn't hold up his work. But it mattered to you. You are the loser, and I'm very much afraid the mate will just write you off and stop trying to help you now.'

'Then what am I to do, sir?'

'That's very plain, too. He thinks you aren't worth the thought and care he's spent on you. Well, we've got to prove to him that you are. You've got to make him believe in you again and that won't be easy.' He stood up and Cam too got to his feet. 'You know, Cam, we all make mistakes and when we are young most of them come from the fact that we tend to see things only from one angle – our own. There are many angles

114

to everything – as many angles as there are folk involved, and the more of them we can see and consider the wiser we are, and the stronger and the clearer and straighter our road. Cut along now and think over what I've said. Try to see old Andy's side, to understand him. And try to make him believe in you again. It's up to you.'

Cam looked at the skipper and swallowed the lump that had come in his throat. 'I'll try, sir,' he said and moved towards the door. 'And thank you, sir. You're – you're a brick!'

Captain Carey waved his hand and smiled. 'Okay. Off you go then, and mind the poltergeist!'

12

THE mass of Curaçao Island was already showing on the horizon when Cam left the captain's cabin, and before he could begin to tell Rusty what had happened, or even get it all clear in his own mind, stations were called and he had to go aft. But all the time he was working there, helping Calamity get up the mooring lines, stripping the hatches, rigging the derricks, oiling and draining the winches, he was thinking and his face showed his thoughts were anything but happy.

Captain Carey's last words had staggered him, for they could only mean one thing – that he had guessed the truth about the haunting of the mate. It was plain he intended to keep what he knew to himself, but that was small comfort. Old Andy was every bit as wide awake and shrewd as the skipper, and what one had deduced the other could also work out. The question was, had old Andy guessed, and, if not, how long would it be before he did so; and then what would he do about it?

Cam brightened up a little as they steamed into the harbour of Willemstad. It was the strangest and most fascinating place he had ever seen. Barbados had been colourful, amazingly pretty; Boca del Sol majestic, and, because of its history, exciting; but this was different. It was fantastic. The entrance was a narrow cleft in a low black cliff and they passed through it into a vast basin like the crater of a burnt-out volcano. It was ringed round with hummocks of jagged black rock, dotted all over with great oil storage tanks, and the town itself was like the pictures he had seen of old Dutch towns – tall half-timbered houses that leaned towards each other across narrow cobbled streets. It was all spotlessly clean, but baked and shimmering in the sun.

They moored alongside a fine concrete wharf with cranes and whitewashed warehouses, which had wide arched doors, like church doors, and low roofs of warm red tiles.

'It's queer,' said Cam as he stared and tried to drink it in. 'Somehow it makes you feel that time has slipped, or stood still or something.' And when they had looked their fill, the boys went below for dinner.

'Well?' demanded Rusty when Cam had ladled out the soup. 'What did he call you back for? About the mate?'

Cam nodded. 'He knows.'

'He knows what?'

'About our poltergeist.'

Rusty dropped his spoon and stared. 'Gosh! Then we're sunk.'

'We're sunk all right, but not in the way you think. He won't say anything or do anything about it, though it strikes me if Ma Carey knows it can only be a matter of time before old Andy guesses too. In fact, I've an idea he knows now. Maybe he knew all along. We've been a pair of chumps, you know, Rusty.'

'You're telling me. But still I can't see how he got wise to it. It looked copper-bottomed to me.'

Cam pushed back his plate. 'I wasn't thinking about that,' he said quietly. 'We were a pair of chumps before we ever thought of a way of getting back at Andy.'

'How do you make that out?'

'We went off half-cocked. The skipper made me see that and I could kick myself all round the deck for not seeing it before.'

Cam went on to repeat as much as he could of what Captain

Carey had said. Some of it was simple enough and had gone right home to him and as he talked, more of it became clear, but Rusty either couldn't or wouldn't see it.

'So what?' he demanded when Cam had finished.

'Well, don't you see what it means? We've had old Andy wrong right from the start.'

Rusty's face screwed up. 'Like stink we have,' he popped. 'I know old Andy, and the skipper jawing you for ten minutes isn't going to make me change my mind about him.'

'Well,' retorted Cam flatly, 'it's made me change mine. And if you weren't so pig-headed you wouldn't talk like that.'

'And might I ask what you're going to do about it now?' Rusty sneered. 'Go crawling round the mate, I suppose, and try to make yourself his little blue-eye!'

Cam flushed angrily and his fists clenched but he held himself in check. 'There's no need to be nasty about it,' he said steadily. 'I'm not doing any crawling. But we've made a mistake and I've got the guts to admit it. As I see it we've given old Andy the idea that we're not worth bothering with. Well, it seems to me plain horse sense for us to try to show him we are.'

'Aw, nuts! You're talking a lot of tripe. How can you do that? You know what he is.'

Cam nodded. 'I know what he is. It won't be easy and I can't see yet even how to start; but I'm going to try.'

Try he did, and desperately hard, but as he had foreseen it wasn't easy.

The work went on and they did their share of it, but it was from the bosun their orders came now and old Andy seemed to have forgotten their existence. And now he had withdrawn from them Cam began to understand for the first time just how big a part he had played in their lives. He hadn't interfered; they had seen very little of him really, but he had been there behind everything they did, watching, measuring their progress, and always ready with a gruff word at just the right moment to help them along. Without this Cam felt lost.

He did consider the possibility of going to the mate and telling him everything – asking him to wipe out the past and let them start afresh; but as Rusty was so fond of saying, talk is cheap and Andy at the best could only say, 'Show me.' So in the end it came back to themselves. They had to show him, and the real problem was how; where to start?

Rusty's attitude didn't make things any easier either, for he wasn't yet convinced that Andy had been doing his best for them on the passage out. They had long and bitter arguments about it and made little headway, and all the time Cam worried away at the problem.

Meanwhile the discharging was completed and orders for the homeward loading came. The ship was to proceed to Cardenas Bay on the north coast of Cuba and load sugar for the United Kingdom. She hummed now with speculation about the final port of destination. Fastnet for orders was the only destination in the charter and that meant either Liverpool or London. In the arguments for and against each place, the poltergeist and all the events of the outward voyage – even the adventure in Boca del Sol – were forgotten.

They were due to sail at day break, and in the evening Cam had one more look at Willemstad, wandering through the narrow crooked streets in bright moonlight and feeling more strongly than ever that time had slipped. He always remembered the place like that – white, silent, fantastic, in the moonlight.

The *Langdale* pulled out in torrential rain next morning and headed northwards across the Caribbean Sea, her course laying up through the Windward Passage – the gap between the islands of Cuba and Haiti – and then west along the

Bahama Channel. Just on a thousand miles it was and they reckoned on doing it in under four days – if the weather held.

'If the weather holds!' croaked Calamity as he shook the rain off his oilskin and mopped his long mournful face when they had finished squaring up the poop. 'You know what I said that night we left Barbados. 'It's against nature.' Right. Well, this is against nature too.' He pointed to the loom of Curaçao Island almost lost in the sheeting rain astern. 'That island is arid. It only rains there about once in seven years and look at it now. Believe me, young Renton, we're for it.'

The sky lifted during the afternoon, however, and Cam, dismissing the old sailor's prophecy as just another bit of his habitual gloom, forgot all about it. His mind was still on the problem of the mate.

Then at supper that night he got a dim idea of what they must do.

They had finished eating and Rusty was sprawling on the settee. 'Well,' he yawned, 'That's another one done, and gosh! I'm fed up with this voyage. The same thing day after day and nothing to do in the evenings but stooge around.'

'You've still got to clear away and wash the pots up,' retorted Cam. 'It's your peggy.'

'Oh, blow the pots! I'll do them in the morning.'

'And what if old Andy takes it into his head to do an inspection?'

Rusty laughed. 'He won't. Not on a short passage like this. He's got other things to think of.'

'You never know. He might.' Cam looked around and saw how untidy the place was. 'And if he did –'

'If he did, he'd blow us up, and who cares about that!'

'Well,' answered Cam, 'I do, if you don't and –' He stopped and a frown puckered his freckled face. 'Jumping snakes, Rusty, I'm a prize idiot!'

'I know that. But what's bitten you now?'

Cam drew a deep breath. 'I'll tell you. I've been racking my brains to find a way of putting us right with the mate and couldn't see where to start, and all the time it's here, right here in our own quarters under our noses.'

'I don't see –'

'Look, man! The mess and everything. Can't you see we've got horribly slack about everything? We're getting into the habit of letting things slide. You don't suppose old Andy misses that, do you? It just fits in with everything else he thinks about us and there's no hope of getting him to change unless we change first.'

Rusty sat up and looked round as if he was seeing the place for the first time. 'Well,' he said slowly, 'now you come to mention it, things are in a bit of muck. Maybe – but a thing like that can't make so much difference.'

'It can!' Cam was convinced now. 'I'm sure it can. All the difference in the world. I see it now. Why do you think we feel bored and fed up in the evening? Just because we're slack. We've got books to work on. Seamanship, trig, navigation – plenty to kill all the time we've got if we were keen – but you can't be keen in a muck-hole; you can't be keen in some things if you're lazy and sloppy in others. Ma Carey said something about things interlocking, working one on the other. Maybe that's what he was getting at.'

Rusty's pug-nosed face was puckered up and his eyes completely closed. 'By gosh, Cam!' he exploded at last. 'Maybe you've hit it. Let's have a go anyhow.' He jumped up and began sliding the supper dishes into the bucket. 'It's my peggy.'

'I'll help you. Then we'll start on *Nichols*. Perhaps the second mate will give us a hand if we ask him. We'll really get stuck into it.'

Rusty picked up the bucket, and made for the door. 'Not

half we won't. And we'll show old Andy what we're made of.'

Such resolutions have often been made and seldom kept, but they were lucky and that evening was the turning-point of the voyage for the boys. The second mate readily agreed to spend half an hour or so of each dog-watch looking over their work. They found the going heavy at first, but they stuck to it and with his help soon got through the dreary stuff of sines and cosines, secants and cotangs, to actual problems in navigation and became absorbed.

Meanwhile the *Langdale* drove north on her course and this time it wasn't only Calamity who worried about the weather. Captain Carey himself kept an anxious eye on the barometer and had the radio operator on the jump all hours, collecting weather reports.

The second day out from Curaçao, after breaking weirdly with streaks and jags of dirty crimson cloud all round the horizon, became overcast before the sun was up, and as the day wore on the heat from an unseen sun became almost unbearable. There was no wind, and yet the air seemed full of a queer, sad soughing as if a wind was there just beyond the ship and couldn't reach her, and sometimes the grey lid of cloud would sag and a little splatter of rain darken the surface of the sea.

'She's brewing up,' croaked Calamity just before noon, and an hour later the warning Captain Carey had been waiting for came over the radio.

Cam was in the wheelhouse cleaning out the flag locker when the radio operator came up with a message, and he heard the skipper read it over to the second mate.

'This is it, Mr. Hartland,' he said. 'A tropical disturbance has developed in the Western Caribbean and is now centred one hundred to hundred and twenty-five miles south of Jamaica, moving north-eastward, attended by shifting gales and winds of hurricane force near the centre. Caution advised Eastern Cuba and Western Haiti.'

'And that,' said Happy Hartland, 'means us.'

Captain Carey sighed. 'I'm afraid so. Looks like it's headed up for the Windward Passage, but if we can keep in front of it till we get round Cape Maysi and into the Bahama Channel we'll be all right. Anyhow that's the only thing we can do. I'll go down to the chief and see if he can squeeze another half knot out of the engines. Keep a good look-out and let me know if the barometer starts playing tricks.'

The skipper went down, and when he had finished his job, Cam stood for a moment in the wing of the bridge where the second mate was keeping his watch. He had seen the frown of anxiety on Captain Carey's face and he was eager to know just what it was that threatened them.

'What's it all about, Mr. Hartland?' he asked. 'And what's a tropical disturbance?'

'I'll show you,' the second mate replied and led the way into the chart room where a great chart of the West Indies was spread out on the table. 'Take a look at that.'

Cam stared eagerly at the chart and saw how the islands, springing in a great arc from the mainland of North America, sweep out into the Atlantic and reach down to the bulge of South America, enclosing the Gulf of Mexico and the Caribbean Sea. They are quite big islands at first – Cuba and Haiti – then they become small and linked up with shoals and coral reefs called cays. Inside the great arc of the islands were one or two small land masses such as Curaçao, Aruba, and, biggest of all, Jamaica. The *Langdale*'s course was drawn on the chart, and Cam saw at a glance that it passed not far from the eastern end of Jamaica.

'Well,' said Hartland, 'a tropical disturbance is just another name for a hurricane and a hurricane isn't just any old gale of wind that pipes up, but something special. They breed in the Caribbean and down on the Spanish Main at this time of year.'

'But how?'

'Something to do with the heat and humidity, I suppose. You get much the same thing in the China Sea but there they are called typhoons; and in the southern states of America they are twisters or cyclones, in the Argentine and Brazil, pamperos. In a very small area the barometric pressure suddenly drops and that forms your storm centre.'

Cam nodded. 'I see. But if this one is south of Jamaica why is the old Man so worried? We can easily get round it.'

'Ah, that's where the catch is, Cam. The storm centre doesn't stay put. It moves – sometimes quickly, sometimes slowly. Usually out here they form far to the south and move in a north-easterly direction out into the Atlantic. But you can't count on that. Some of them swing right back and bust across the Central American isthmus; some go north and do terrible damage in Florida and the southern states; some strike along the islands.'

Then Hartland turned to the chart and showed Cam how the Caribbean was really a vast lake with few gaps in its outer ring through which a ship of the *Langdale*'s size could navigate.

'So you see,' he concluded, 'we've either got to head south and west and steam all round Cuba, in which case we'd be going towards the storm centre and in a fine pickle if it curved back; or hold on to our course in the path of the storm and hope we can get round the corner before it reaches us. If it catches us up while we are in the Windward Passage – well, it will be just too bad.'

Cam went down off the bridge and a little later he noticed the quickened beat of the engine, and knew the chief engineer had responded to the captain's appeal.

'Holy smoke!' said Calamity at supper time. 'Feel the old girl shake. She's never been driven like this before.'

When the meal was over the crowd gathered as usual on the cross-bunker hatch but there was no sing-song. Nightfall had brought no drop in the temperature, and the men lay around in little groups feeling the air press on them like damp flannel hot out of an oven. By this time everybody in the ship knew about the hurricane and why Captain Carey was racing up for the Windward Passage.

Would she make it? Would the engines stand the strain? These two questions were in everyone's mind and they watched and waited in silence – even Calamity Calshot forgetting for once his part as a prophet of disaster. They watched the sea and the sky; they stared ahead for the first blink of Cape Maysi light; they felt the vibration, counted the engine-beat, and no one thought of turning in.

The night had begun black and completely overcast, but about ten o'clock the lid of cloud suddenly split right overhead and all the eastern half of it rolled away, showing the moon, hazy with heat, and the hard mass of Haiti wide on the starboard bow. The western sky remained solidly packed with black cloud. The upper edge of it was sharp and seemed to pass right over the mastheads as though the ship was sailing along the threshold of an immense and terrifying cavern. The vague rustle of the wind that had plagued them all day grew to a whisper, and the great upflung flares of heat lightning, blue and weird, leapt behind the clouds. The silence was tense.

Then suddenly on it the voice of the look-out man rang out. 'Light ahead, sir. Half point on the port bow.'

There was a rush to the rail. Would it be Cape Maysi or just another ship. They stared and stared, then Cam picked it up. It blinked.

'There it is. It's Cape Maysi all right and we've made it!'

They had made it, but it was a near thing, and as he said the words the whisper of the wind changed to a subdued hiss which grew rapidly to a wild shriek as it struck the ship like a wall. She staggered and heeled under the impact, then drove on, and as she went the lightning leapt from the cloud-edge to the sea.

This was no flare of blue heat lightning, but forked and white and terrifying. It struck the sea not a hundred yards from the port quarter, reaching out like a tendril towards the moon, then bending in to the water with a crack like a whip.

It was followed in an instant by a rattle of thunder which almost split the eardrums of the watching men. For a moment they were dazed and stared at each other stupidly, then the cloud opened and the rain came down in ropes.

An hour later they were round the Cape into the Bahama Channel, and each turn of the engines increased the distance between them and the storm that for a while had pressed them so closely.

13

ALTHOUGH Captain Carey continued to be anxious about the weather, the *Langdale* arrived at Cardenas without further alarms and, threading her way through the maze of cays which encloses the shallow bay and makes it a lagoon, anchored just before noon about three miles from the town.

With the memory of all the tear and bustle of unloading fresh in his mind, Cam rather expected to see thousands of tons of cargo stacked ready and at least half a dozen gangs of men standing by to hurl it on board; but to his surprise the lagoon, which was all of ten miles long, seemed deserted, and neither on the ragged shoreline nor the encircling cays – both densely grown with low shrub – was there any sign of life. The whole place was so eerily still, so desolate in its silence, he thought for a moment the skipper had made a mistake and brought them into the wrong lagoon.

Then the second mate put him wise. 'The one thing that's necessary in the Cuban sugar trade,' he said, 'is patience. We might be here a month and then have to go to a deepwater port like Havana or Caibarien for another week to finish. It all depends on the weather and how the sugar comes down from the back country.'

In the end the second mate's guess was proved to be a long way wide of the mark, but even so they lay sixteen days in Cardenas Bay and for the first five of them didn't see a single bag of sugar.

At first Cam hated the place. It reminded him too much of Port of Spain and those things connected with the outward passage which he was trying so hard to live down and wipe out. And besides this, he missed the cargo work – the rush and rattle, the drive and sweat, and the sense of achievement that came from creating order out of confusion. He felt at a loose end and rather lost for a while.

Not that they were idle. Old Andy saw the slack spell as a chance to catch up on the maintenance work; he aimed to give the ship at least one coat of paint from truck to water-line before she sailed for home, and the deck crew, Cam and Rusty with them, were busy all the time slapping it on. This painting itself could be exciting enough, especially when they were doing the masts and funnel and had to perform all manner of gymnastic feats in a bosun's chair, but there wasn't the same thrill in it. It didn't call for judgment and decisions as the cargo work did, and without his realizing it, that part of the job had come to mean a lot to Cam.

However he shook down to it after a couple of days, and then discovered the lagoon wasn't nearly so desolate as he had imagined.

The town itself was at the western end and hidden in the scrub, but there were buildings on some of the outlying cays. These were in the main the holiday homes of the planters from up country. They were white and pink and pale blue, and seen across the flat surface of the water, shimmering in the heat, looked more like decorations off a Christmas tree than real houses.

Then all day long small craft – launches, fast outboard motor boats, and all manner of little sailing vessels – were nosing in and out of the hidden creeks along the shore line.

And finally there were the pelicans. From daybreak till dark they floated and flapped around the ship and Cam never tired of watching them. They were comical birds – so pompous, so self-important, and so amazingly clumsy. They would rise from the water with a tremendous flapping of wings and, getting up as high as the masthead, sail round with their necks drawn into their shoulders and their great beaks sticking out as if they were pieces of heavy luggage they carried around and might leave somewhere any minute. Then one of them would spot a fish and down would go his beak, up his tail, and he would drop like a stone and disappear in a shower of spray and broken water.

So one way and another the five days passed and at last the cargo began to arrive. It came off in sailing lighters, and as the wind blew steadily from east to west along the lagoon it was quite a job for them to make the ship. The longshoremen handled the craft like yachts, tacking out in fine style, and all the time they lay there Cam never saw a single one of them miss stays. Out they would come, heeling over to the wind and butting the spray high, holding on as if they would drive clean over the cays and into the Atlantic; then, with the shoal water right under the bows the skipper would put down the tiller and round she would come, smoothly as a gull, and away on the other tack.

Once a lighter was alongside, the stevedore's gang made quick work of emptying it. The sugar was in sacks—seven to the ton – and each lighter carried about a thousand. It was hoisted aboard in rope slings, seven bags to the lift, lowered down the hold, then stowed, each sack being carried and dropped into place by hand.

It was terribly heavy work, and Cam, tallying the bags as they came in at number two hold, marvelled how the men could stand under the weight, let alone go on throwing the three-hundred-and-twenty-pound sacks about for hours at a stretch.

But the cargo came slowly. On some days no more than two lighters made the trip, and the days mounted up. With

*

about three thousand tons aboard she moved out to deeper anchorage nine miles from the town, and the longer beat against the wind made the flow of sugar even less certain and slower.

Once he had settled down to it, Cam didn't mind the delay and, eager as he was now to drive ahead with his navigation and theoretical seamanship, he saw every hour they spent waiting for cargo as so much more time for study, and used it. Rusty took it hard but he too was keen now, and determined to prove himself to old Andy. They worked together – sometimes in the chart room where the second mate set them problems on obsolete charts and helped them all he could, but mostly under the awning on the poop where they could watch the lagoon and see the lighters come sailing out towards the ship.

The boys were happy – happier than they had been since leaving Liverpool – and the only thing that worried them was uncertainty about the mate. All the way from Boca del Sol he had completely ignored them, and by neither word nor look had he given any hint of what he was thinking about them. Each night when they turned in and put out the light, their talk came back to him, what they had seen of him, what he had done, how he had looked; Rusty was as eager as Cam to know, for by this time he too was convinced they had been wrong about old Andy on the voyage out.

But if the mate noticed the change in the boys he gave no sign.

At first they wondered if he knew about their studying, if perhaps the second mate had mentioned to him that he was coaching them in trig and navigation; that kept them going, but gradually they became absorbed and fascinated by the work, and in the end reached a point where that itself was sufficient and they would have gone on with it, mate or no mate.

At the nine-mile anchorage the sing-songs which for various reasons had stopped after Port of Spain were resumed, and again the crowd lay around on the cross-bunker hatch in the moonlight and talked while the cook, his apron tucked into his belt, strummed on the banjo till he struck the tune that would start them singing. Cam never forgot those evenings. It was good to lie there with one day's work behind him and another ahead; good to watch the clouds sailing endlessly across the moon, to see the shore lights flicker and hear the faint far-off sounds from the houses on the cays; good to see the men around him and to feel himself accepted as one of them, as a sailor who could pull his weight and stand his turn in anything that might come along.

The songs they sang in Cardenas Lagoon were different – quiet, sad little songs, and half-forgotten capstan and mainsail-haul shanties – and under the peace and contentment, they were restless, impatient to be out and away again.

'How much did we load today, young Renton?' Calamity asked one night.

'Two thousand bags,' Cam replied, and Calamity groaned and spat in a wide arc across the deck into the scuppers.

'Two thousand bags! Suffering smoke, we'll be here till we go aground on our beef bones at this rate.'

Then Bandy took him up.

'The trouble with you, Calamity, is you're never satisfied. You're like all old shellbacks. When you're home you want to be away and as soon as you've dropped the pilot, you're hankering to be back. You should get yourself a job on the Liverpool ferries.'

'It isn't that, man,' put in Taffy, 'but the lying around. Every day is exactly the same as the one before and the one that will come after. What we want is a change – something to happen that we are not expecting.'

'We're always getting that,' retorted Calamity. 'When we left Liverpool we didn't expect to come to Cuba, and when we arrived here we didn't expect to be so long loading. We don't know yet when we'll finish or when we'll sail; what sort of passage we'll make or where we'll fetch in the end. Maybe that's what keeps us sailing – the fact that at sea you never know what lies ahead.'

This time Bandy agreed. 'True enough!' he said. 'It's always the unexpected, the thing nobody counted on, that comes at sea.'

Although the hurricane they had escaped so narrowly in the Windward Passage had disappeared and blown itself out in the Atlantic, the weather was still uncertain. Two new storm centres developed while they lay at Cardenas. The first was spotted just a little north of Barbados and swept swiftly in a shallow curve west to pass inland across the southern part of Mexico; but the second was more serious. It formed south of Jamaica and moving slowly north-eastward threatened the eastern end of Cuba for days. Cardenas was well out of its track, but there was always the danger of it striking back along the coast, and the skipper was impatient to be away from the shoals and cays into deep water where he would have room to run and dodge if necessary.

Meanwhile, because of the hurricane weather, the air in the lagoon was stifling. Under the blaze of the sun the steel fabric of the ship became so hot that by midday it was painful to touch a rail or hatch coaming with the naked hand; and night-fall brought so little change that the decks were hardly cool before the sun was on them again.

'Gosh!' said Rusty as they turned in that night. 'What wouldn't I give for a long cold drink! Remember the ices we had the night before we sailed from Liverpool? Oh boy, oh boy!'

Cam threw a pillow at him and climbed into his bunk. 'There's plenty of water in the pump,' he said, and Rusty groaned.

'I know, I know. But it's warm and it's sticky and it tastes of that foul stuff Andy puts in the tank to keep it pure.'

'Well, never mind,' Cam chaffed as he put out the light, 'you'll be cool enough, you stiff, before we get home. Wait till we're on the great circle for the Fastnet and it's blowing a northerly gale with snow and hail squalls. You'll be longing for Cardenas then.'

Lying in the dark, they talked on drowsily until the faint sounds from the shore and even the nearer ship noises had died away and they fell asleep about midnight.

Two hours later they were awakened by a tremendous explosion which shook the ship from stem to stern and seemed to hurl them out of their bunks.

Cam snapped on the light and for a moment they stared at each other, dazed with sleep and the shock of the violent awakening; then Rusty pointed to the porthole through which the night could be seen full of red glare.

'Suffering snakes! She's on fire,' he yelled, and made for the door.

'Not in your bare feet, you chump!' shouted Cam.

They dragged on their sea-boots, then ran down the alley-way leading on to the bridge-deck. As they went they became aware of a great roaring noise and at the open door stopped aghast at what they saw. About ten feet from the door coaming was a small square hatch through which the coal was trimmed into the after end of the 'tween-deck bunker. Usually it was covered and neatly battened down but now it gaped wide open and out of it a column of flame shot twenty feet into the air, roaring like a blast furnace.

Cam gripped Rusty's arm. 'We'd better get the fire-hose

rigged,' he shouted. 'You nip down below and get the donkey-man to start the pump on the deck-service line and I'll run it out and couple up.'

Shielding their faces from the searing heat with upraised arms, the boys doubled round the corner of the house, and while Rusty sped below into the engine-room Cam dragged a length of hose off the reel under the boat-skids and began to hammer the cap off the nearest coupling with the heel of his sea-boot.

His ears were getting used now to the roar, and under it he heard the pounding of feet on the deck plates as the sailors and firemen came tumbling out of the quarters aft; but before the first of them had arrived he had the hose connected and then, with the nozzle in his hands ready, he tried to estimate the extent of the fire while he waited for the water.

The heat from the pillar of flame was intense and already the paint on the bulkheads nearest to it was blistering and smoking under it; but the immediate danger seemed to be from the burning fragments of the shattered hatch-boards which had a number of minor blazes going already on the boat-covers and skids where they had fallen.

By the time the beat of the pump picked up and the water came kicking powerfully out of the nozzle, Cam had decided that first he must check those secondary outbreaks, for he saw clearly, if they were left, the whole midships section of the ship could be ablaze in a few minutes.

Bracing himself against the backward thrust of the hose he tackled the boat-covers, and was working round to the top of the engine-room casing when Calamity Calshot and Bandy Bascombe suddenly appeared through the drifting smoke and without a word added the strength of their big hands to the struggle.

Cam explained briefly what he was doing and Calamity nodded approvingly.

'That's the idea, young Renton. Stop it spreading,' he said. 'Leave it to us now and have a blow.'

Obediently, Cam dropped back and joined the group of men clustered round old Andy and the chief engineer in the mouth of the alley-way.

The mate's face as usual was expressionless but the chief looked worried.

'I knew that coal, baking under the hot decks, was generating a lot of gas, but I'd hoped it was getting away through the ventilators,' he said.

The mate grunted. 'From the way it blew up there must have been quite a bit of pressure there. What do you reckon touched it off? None of your men in there with duck lamps, I suppose?'

The chief shook his head. 'No. We've been working from the lower 'tween-deck. It must have been a spark from a faulty electric cable. What do you think of it?'

'We'll never get it out from above. The flame is coming out of the hatch all right, but the question is, where's the heart of it?' He frowned, then his head shot out towards the chief. 'That's it, chief. We'll have to get a couple of gangs of men down there and throw the coal back till we can reach the burning section and get a hose on it.'

'But,' the chief objected, 'it will be terrible down there – the heat and the fumes. And dangerous too. There may be other pockets of gas and you'll never know when they might blow back on you.'

'Dangerous all right,' grunted old Andy, 'but short of scuttling the ship it's the only way. We'll see what the men feel about it.'

Leaving Bandy and Calamity on the hose, he called the rest

of the crew around him and told them his plan, explaining the danger and difficulty involved, then called for volunteers. Not a single man hung back, and while the bosun and carpenter went forrard for shovels he led the way down the engine room, through the alley-way between the boilers into the stokehold, then up the ladders into the empty fore-end of the burning bunker.

They carried with them a special gas-proof electric lamp with a long flexible lead, and under its yellow light the face of the coal gleamed, but apart from the stifling heat there was no sign of the fire.

Andy measured the width of the bunker with a glance, then turned to the men.

'We'll have to shift anything up to a hundred tons,' he said, 'and we'd best work in relays. Three men on the face throwing it back as far as they can; another three pitching it back from where it lands the first time; and another three behind them. That's nine men to start with. The rest had better get up into the fresh air until it's time to relieve the first lot. Short bursts. We should be able to stick a fifteen minutes' spell.'

Sorting themselves out into gangs of three with a stokehold hand in each squad, they set to and soon nine shovels were scraping and thumping and the close air of the bunker became heavy with the dust they raised.

Cam, who was in the second squad with Bandy and a wiry little Scotch fireman, working just behind the mate and Calamity, started off at a tremendous rate. He was keyed up with excitement and the shovel felt like a toy in his grip. But after about five minutes he was panting, and Bandy, stopping a moment to spit on his hands, threw him a sharp glance.

'Take it steady, son,' he grunted. 'You'll kill yourself at that rate.'

He stooped to the job again and Cam, watching him, quickly realized there was more to shovelling coal than he had ever imagined. Bandy worked rhythmically, using the swing of his body and the shape of the shovel to ease the weight. Trying to keep time with him, Cam gradually got the knack and, breathing easier now, felt he could go on for hours.

He was surprised when the quarter-hour was up, but when he got out on deck for his breather and felt the night air pouring into his lungs, he realized just how bad conditions were in the bunker.

The second spell below was worse than the first. There was still no sign of the fire, but now little curls and puffs of thick yellow smoke were coming out of the coal, and the acrid reek of sulphur was added to the choking dust and baking heat in which they worked. When he was relieved this time he was coughing, the muscles in his back and legs were aching, and, worst of all, his hands were beginning to blister. Rusty, working further back, was still full of go, but Calamity, who had been in the thick of it with old Andy, was in a bad way. They were all black with coal dust and looked a weird sight with only the whites of their eyes gleaming in the glare of the fire.

Sitting in a row on the deck with their backs against the bulkhead, they let their bodies grow slack and only looked up to gulp down the mugs of scalding black coffee the cook kept circulating among them. When, all too quickly, the rest period was over and they got to their feet, Calamity staggered and, but for Cam putting his shoulder against him, would have fallen. But when Bandy suggested he should take another spell, Calamity turned on him fiercely and told him to look after his own affairs.

'I'm as good a man as you are!' he snarled, 'and if you can stick it so can I.'

They went on into the bunker again and for a while Calamity

worked as if his strength had suddenly been doubled. But it was only the pride of him and his indomitable will, and suddenly, without a sound, he pitched head first into the coal.

At a sign from the mate, Bandy and Rusty dragged the old sailor out and carried him up on deck, while Cam moved forward and picking up his shovel worked shoulder to shoulder with Andy.

The sulphur fumes were thickening now, and soon they had to stop to wrap wet cloths round their faces. At the same time Andy had the hose brought down and, by having it played constantly on the coal, managed to check the stifling dust a little.

They drove themselves to it again and Cam lost count of time as he shovelled. The ache in his legs and back no longer troubled him. It was still there but he had become numbed to it and the only thing he felt was the shovel, dragging at his hands, burning and sticking where the skin had rubbed off the broken blisters and the raw flesh was oozing blood.

So through the night they toiled. How many more spells he had on deck he never knew, but he felt each one of them would be the last, that he would never be able to drag himself to his feet again once he sat down. Yet he went on and on, for he knew dimly that old Andy too was going on, and he was determined that he wouldn't give up until the mate had cried enough.

His one fear was that his weary body would defeat his will and let him down as Calamity's had done, but when the grey of the dawn began to creep up the eastern sky and show the dim loom of the shore-line and the distant cays, he was still there, still swinging his shovel and staring with smarting smoke-reddened eyes at the endless coal that still smoked evilly.

And in the end it was his shovel that finally broke through to the fire. He himself was too far gone to notice it, but Andy caught the first red glow.

'Stand back there!' he croaked. 'We've made it. Where's that hose?'

They left it then to a fresher squad and the rest was easy. By breakfast time the fire was out.

But neither Cam nor Rusty knew anything about that. Blackened with sweat-caked coal dust and smelling abominably of sulphur and fire, they were sleeping stretched out on the deck in their quarters; and the last thing each of them remembered as he lay down and let himself go into the dark emptiness of sleep was old Andy's words to them as they came out of the bunker for the last time and he saw who it was that had worked beside him.

'So it was you two!' he whispered. 'I always knew you were the breed.'

14

RUSTY, in spite of his rather indolent ways, was wiry, and after six hours' sleep and a hot bath he was none the worse for the struggle in the burning bunker. It was different with Cam. He was, if anything, tougher than Rusty and got rid of his weariness and aches as quickly, but his hands were in a bad way. Andy himself, his banana-like fingers sure and clever as a surgeon's and gentle as a woman's, cleaned and bandaged them for him, and then forbade him to handle anything heavier than a pencil till they were healed.

This meant Cam did no more cargo work while the *Langdale* was loading, and instead of sweating down the hold he spent the rest of the time the ship was on the Cuban coast doing little jobs for the second mate in the chart-room.

Under the circumstances, no one would have blamed him if he had laid up and done nothing till he could shed the bandages, but he saw the release from tallying as a golden opportunity and he made good use of every minute of the time.

For him, the chart-room was the most interesting place in the ship. The engine-room might be the heart of it, but here was the brain, the nerve centre from which her movements were controlled.

At first sight it wasn't much of a place – a fair-sized square cabin with a door at each side and a long window across the fore end through which the officer of the watch could look forrard past the man at the wheel. There was a very wide, elbow-high table under this window, a settee along the after end with a long bookshelf over it, a clock, an aneroid barometer, a thermometer, and two or three framed diagrams and certificates on the bulkheads, and that was all.

And even the fact that the long drawers under the high table held scores of charts and such things as parallel rulers and protractors, that the padded locker on the starboard side held the chronometer – a clock so wonderfully made it lost only a tenth of a second a day – didn't seem to amount to very much. But Cam already saw these things as the tools of his trade, and in those last few days at Cardenas and the rushed week-end at Matanzas where the *Langdale* finally finished loading, they became more than that, even.

As he became familiar with the purpose of each piece of equipment he began to understand how it linked up with the rest to form a wonderfully efficient weapon with which Captain Carey, old Andy, and Hartland fought the sea and gale and fog; a strong, sure shield against the dangers of shoal and tide-rip and hidden reef; and his eagerness to use it himself grew with his understanding, the one feeding the other till he could hardly tear himself away from it all to eat.

His time was mostly taken up correcting charts. These are made by the Admiralty and give not only the outline of the coasts but also the lights and buoys, the main landmarks and the shape and nature of the sea-bed in the area they cover. They also mark every shoal and reef; every dangerous wreck, the main currents, and a whole mass of detail which might be of use to the sailor. A great deal of this information changes from time to time – buoys are shifted, the character of lights altered, new wrecks appear and old ones fall to pieces or are salvaged and so on – and shipmasters are advised of each change in an Admiralty Notice to Mariners. When these notices are urgent they are broadcast by radio, but even so they are constantly accumulating and somehow the second mate has to find time to deal with them.

Being keen to learn, Cam soon picked up the knack of printing tiny letters and figures neatly, and once he had it Happy Hartland left him to it.

So with the time passing more quickly than ever, he worked away while the loading went on and the *Langdale* sat deeper in the water every day.

At last she could take no more at Cardenas without going aground, and when Captain Carey had made a final trip ashore to square accounts with the agent and sign the bills of lading, the anchor was hove up and she sailed in the last of the daylight for Matanzas – a deep-water port a few hours further along the coast.

Standing on the bridge-deck with Rusty, Cam took a last long look at Cardenas.

'Well!' said Rusty. 'Thanks be we're out of that dog-hole at last. Of all the one-eyed dumps a ship could go to that's about the worst.'

But Cam, staring astern, was not so sure. Already the purple shadows were stealing over the lagoon, hiding the shore line and blurring the hills beyond; the lights of the town glimmered vaguely, and even the nearer cays seemed unreal as if they had become detached and floated in a low mist; and somehow it all seemed a little sad. He sighed.

'I don't know,' he said slowly. 'How long have we been here now?'

'Sixteen days, and it seems like half a lifetime. Gosh! It will be great to be homeward bound again.'

'Sixteen days!' Cam echoed. 'It doesn't seem like that to me.'

And this strange feeling of time having speeded up so the days flashed by stayed with him for a long while. In Matanzas the *Langdale* moored alongside a jetty and they were able to go ashore each evening, but the hours spent wandering along the dim-lit streets made little impression on Cam, and for him Cuba always remained the lagoon at Cardenas – the low scrub-covered hills, the cays unreal as a mirage, the long stretch of shimmering water, and the white-sailed lighters beating out across it to the nine-mile anchorage.

Meanwhile old Andy continued to ignore them. Except for his gruff words of approval croaked to them both as they came out of the bunker on the night of the fire, and a few unintelligible grunts as he dressed Cam's hands, he had made no sign to either of them since Boca del Sol, which now seemed so far back as to belong to another voyage. They were still working hard at their navigation and theoretical seamanship, and the deeper they got into it the more completely it absorbed them. Sometimes Cam looking back would remember how in the beginning they had driven themselves to it 'just to show old Andy', and then he would marvel they could ever have needed such a spur. It wasn't only the fact that he felt himself going ahead at his job; that was important, but there was something else to it as well. There was the thrill of solving a difficult problem and a feeling that he was growing as the thick volume of nautical tables became understandable to him, and the movements of the sun and stars became not merely things that happened but things that he himself could measure and calculate.

In spite of all this, however, they still wondered about the mate – what he was thinking, how much he noticed, if he had forgotten Boca del Sol and all that had happened on the outward passage – and the night the last of the cargo came aboard in Matanzas, they were talking about him in their cabin.

'If you ask me,' said Rusty, 'we cooked our goose with Andy at Boca del Sol. He's a queer old bird, you know, and terribly pig-headed.'

Cam stretched out his legs and shoved his hands deep into his trousers pockets. 'I'm not so sure,' he began thoughtfully, then stopped.

'Not so sure of what?'

'That he is pig-headed. He's queer all right, but –'

Rusty's face screwed up. 'You don't know him,' he popped. 'Ask Calamity. He's sailed with him for years and knows him inside out. He's made his mind up about you and me and nothing will make him change it now. I'd like to bet he's already sent a report in to the shore superintendent and we'll be for it when we get home.'

Cam looked up. 'Sacked, you mean?'

'Well, no. We're apprentices bound for four years and we can't be just kicked out like that; but we'll be told to pack our bags and transfer to another ship, you'll see.'

There was silence in the room for a few minutes, then suddenly Cam shot the question:

'Would you mind?'

Rusty jerked up his head. 'Me! Fancy asking a stupid question like that after all I've said about the old coot! Why should I mind?'

'Well, I'm asking you,' persisted Cam. 'Would you mind? I would. I don't want to leave the old *Langdale*.'

And this time Rusty flung away and began fingering the books on the shelf above the chest. 'I don't either, and I'd mind an awful lot,' he said quickly. 'But it won't make any difference. I reckon we're sunk.'

Cam stared out through the open porthole. 'Maybe, but –' he began, then before he could say what was in his mind there came a light tap on the door. 'Come in,' he called, and what he wanted to say was never said for the door opened and in walked old Andy himself.

'It's time you boys were in your bunks,' he said huskily, then to Cam: 'How's the hands?'

Cam held them out. He had discarded the bandages that morning. 'Okay now, sir.'

'Good. You know we're sailing at daybreak?'

'Yes, sir.'

'Right, then. I'm putting you on watches for the passage home. Roberts in the port, Renton in the starboard. This will be your last full night in this voyage, so make the most of it and get turned in. That's all.' Then old Andy was gone, closing the door softly behind him.

For a moment the boys stared at each other unbelieving; Rusty's eyes were goggling, then suddenly his face screwed up, but Cam found his tongue first.

'Whippee-ee-ee!' he yelled.

'Whippee-ee-ee!' echoed Rusty, then linking arms they waltzed wildly round the tiny cabin till they were breathless.

The *Langdale* cleared Matanzas in the grey light of the next day's dawn and, threading her way through the cays and reefs into the deep water of the Atlantic, started on the long run homeward.

Her port of discharge was still uncertain. It could be Greenock, Liverpool, or London and her instructions were to proceed to the Fastnet for orders, which meant that some time on the passage she would be given a destination by radio.

This uncertainty, however, couldn't spoil the 'homeward bound' feeling that ran right through the ship the moment the Cuban pilot was dropped, and the men went about their work with a kind of cheerful briskness that was completely new to Cam. Only Calamity Calshot chose to be gloomy. 'We aren't home yet by a long chalk!' he said. 'And if you ask me we're far too deep loaded for my fancy.'

'Oh, stow it, Calamity!' laughed Bandy. 'I'll tell you what. I'll bet you four plugs of baccy we're in Liverpool eighteen days from now.'

'It might not be Liverpool,' put in Taffy.

'And it's late in the year. We'll get equinoctial gales and head winds all the way. Twenty-eight days is nearer the mark, if we make it in that,' croaked Calamity.

But for the first three days the weather was perfect and the ship rattled along in fine style. Her course lay north and east on a vast curve across the Atlantic, and once the purple shadow of Cuba had dipped below the sea rim astern, they would see nothing more but an occasional ship until they raised the Fastnet light on the south-west corner of Ireland.

Cam had for watch-mates Bandy Bascombe and Taffy. The watches were four-hour spells – midnight to 4 a.m. was called the middle or graveyard watch; 4 a.m. to 8 a.m. the morning watch; 8 a.m. till noon the forenoon watch; noon to 4 p.m. the afternoon watch; and to give each group of men the various watches in turn, the 4 till 8 p.m. period was split into two dog-watches.

The main job was the wheel and each man took it in turn for two hours; but from sunset till sunrise there was also the look-out to do, so in the night watches there was one man at the wheel, one on the look-out, and one standing by. A two-hour trick is long enough for anybody to do and the stand-bys and look-outs were specially arranged to make sure a man always went to the wheel fresh. So the man with the ten to twelve wheel did the eight to nine look-out and the nine to ten stand-by; the one with the eight to ten wheel did the ten to eleven stand-by and the eleven to twelve look-out; and the one who had no wheel that watch did the first and last hours stand-by and the middle look-out.

Cam quickly got the hang of it and settled down to the routine. At first the short spells of sleep were a trial and he had to fight himself hard to get out of his bunk when called. But there was a sort of rhythm to the life and when he got into it the question of sleep troubled him no more.

He loved the stand-bys in the galley and the look-outs on the fo'c's'le head, standing right in the eyes of the ship, feeling her lift and surge, hearing the long swish of the bow wave and seeing it roll out away from her forefoot gleaming with phosphorescent light; watching the stars and the masthead swinging slowly against them. But best of all he loved the wheel. To stand there on the grating watching the swaying compass card in the lighted binnacle, feeling the ship under his hands, trying to sense her movements before they started so he could check them and keep the wide wake stretching astern straight and true as a line drawn with a ruler, made him feel good – eight thousand tons of metal and wood and the great beating engine at its heart, in his hands, obeying his will. It was something for a boy of his age to think of; it was achievement and thrill enough to satisfy a grown man, let alone a youngster.

Then the night tricks with the lights all shielded and only the glow from the binnacle thrown up in his face and the vague radiance of the foremast headlight and the sidelights in the velvet darkness; these and the far-off stars and the stillness on which the engine beat like a mighty pulse – the night tricks he loved best of all, and once more he found the days slipping by almost too quickly.

But this time Calamity's forebodings proved well grounded. The fine spell carried them clear of the dangerous hurricane area and then, when they were in the latitude of Bermuda but far to the east of it, the barometer began to fall.

At first that was the only sign of the change and Cam saw nothing to worry about in it, but in the afternoon watch the second mate drew his attention to the heavier swell rolling down on them out of the north-west where the clear-cut line of the horizon had blurred with mist.

'There's something big behind this,' he said, 'and it's a bad sign when the glass falls slowly.'

By nightfall the wind had freshened considerably and the swell was heavier still. As the *Langdale* was steering almost north-east she had it broad on the beam, and long before midnight was rolling heavily and scooping great sullen masses of green water aboard all along her port side.

Cam had the middle watch that night and when he turned out at twelve o'clock to take the first look-out he found he had to do it on the bridge, for the fore-deck was continually awash, and every now and then she was dipping her bows right under.

The wind, however, was still a little south of west and no more than moderate, and he went to the wheel at four bells wondering why there was such a sea with so little wind.

Then soon after he saw the stars blotted out as if a black curtain had been drawn across the sky. At the same time his quick ear caught a low moaning noise under the sough of the wind. There was a splatter of rain. The sky was split with great jags of lightning, and while the thunder was still rumbling and rolling away to the south, the wind suddenly shifted and came away at full gale force out of the north-west.

For the rest of his trick Cam sweated at the wheel. The *Langdale*, steaming along the line of the swell, rolled wildly, and he grew dizzy watching the swinging card in the compass bowl while he tried to hold her on her course.

At seven bells with half an hour of the watch to go, the second mate decided it was dangerous to carry on any longer. He told Cam to bring her up head to wind and sea and sent the stand-by man to call Captain Carey, who approved what had been done and rang the engines down to slow ahead so her speed dropped until she carried only steerage way.

So when Cam handed over to his relief, the ship was hove to – no longer headed home and driving on her course at a steady ten knots, but headed north-west into the wind and fighting to hold her own against the mounting gale and sea.

The gale lasted three days and it was only the beginning. It eased for an hour or two, then swung back into the south-west. This time Captain Carey tried to run before it, but again the sea became too high and once more they hove to.

Even Atlantic gales, however, have an end and this one blew itself out at last. Captain Carey put the *Langdale* back on her course and, still fighting the wild sea the storm had left in its wake, she started to drive homewards again, the thin film of green slime on her decks telling the story of the wet passage she was making.

The sea dropped a good deal that day and by nightfall she was running easier. Everybody on board hoped then they had seen the last of discomfort and excitement for that voyage, and in the dog-watch the talk turned back to speculation on port of destination and arrival day.

When Cam went on to the bridge for the last spell of lookout before the next day broke, the black pall of cloud overhead had broken and through the rift he saw the stars that had been hidden so long. For a moment he looked up at them trying to pick out the ones he knew, then he dropped his eyes and stared ahead where the first flush of day was making the horizon faintly luminous.

The light grew steadily and the navigation lights paled

against it. Soon the foremast stood out clearly and the fo'c's'le head rails gleamed ghost-like as the bows lifted to a sea.

Then suddenly Cam stiffened and stared. There, wide on the starboard bow but no more than two miles off, was a ship. For a moment he couldn't believe his eyes, for he had seen no lights and he should have spotted her long before. It was almost as if she had grown out of the dawn. Then he saw she was carrying no lights and pulling himself together he sang out to the mate.

'Ship on the starboard bow, sir. Close in.'

Old Andy, up in the port wing of the bridge, swung round and stared in turn, then, snatching at the telescope, came hurrying across.

'She's showing no lights, sir,' Cam explained as the mate levelled the long glass. 'I was staring right at her when she loomed up out of the darkness.'

Old Andy grunted, then suddenly he put up the glass and turned to Cam.

'Something queer about that craft. She's not only showing no lights but she's stopped and I can't see anybody on her bridge. Nip down and call the skipper.'

Cam dashed off, and as he went down the ladder he heard the clang of the telegraph as the mate rang the engines to stand by and the rattle of the wheel engine as he put down the helm to come round and investigate the mysterious stranger.

15

WHEN Cam came out on deck again after calling the skipper, the gap between the two ships had narrowed, and the stranger lay revealed in the growing light so close the name and port of registry on her stern could be read with the naked eye.

She was the *Arno* of Galveston – a ship about the same size as the *Langdale* and, like her, deeply laden.

'What do you make of her?' Captain Carey asked, coming on to the bridge right at the heels of Cam.

The mate grunted. His face was as wooden as ever, but there was a gleam of excitement in his eye and the knuckles of his great fists showed white through the tan where they gripped the dodger stay.

'She's derelict. That much is certain. I've had my eye on her ever since we picked her up and not seen a soul.'

'Better make sure of that. Try a long blast on the whistle, Cam.'

Springing across the bridge, Cam lay back on the lanyard and the blare of the siren shattered the morning stillness; but there was no response from the *Arno*.

Captain Carey pulled at his lips. 'She looks very deep forrard and listed to starboard. Come round her stern and let us have a look at the other side of her.'

Andy rapped out an order to Bandy at the wheel, and shouldering the still heavy sea the *Langdale* came round. As she did so and the starboard side of the derelict came in sight, the mate whistled through his teeth, for just abaft the fore-mast they could see a great gash in the *Arno*'s side.

'That's it, I reckon. She's been in collision and the other fellow must have taken off her crew when she started to settle by the head. Probably tried to stand by her but lost touch in that last gale.' Old Andy pushed back his cap and scratched his head. 'What beats me is why she's still afloat with a hole like that in her side.'

Captain Carey shook his head. 'It can't be as bad as it looks or she's got a lot of timber in her cargo forrard. That's it. She hails from Galveston, so likely enough she's loaded with general cargo from the Gulf ports – cotton and hog's hair; hickory logs and Honduras redwood. You know the stuff. Lots of buoyancy in all of it.' He picked up the binoculars and carefully searched the horizon.

Meanwhile the excitement old Andy was holding in check had spread through the ship. Cam felt it growing. Although it was yet so early, all hands were out and they gathered in little groups on the bridge-deck, staring across the tumbled grey sea and all talking eagerly about the derelict.

By the age-old law of the sea once a ship has been abandoned by her crew, both she and her cargo belong to whoever can board her and take her to a safe port. It is a chance that seldom comes, for the seaman's struggle against the sea is continuous and he never gives up until the last flicker of hope is gone. But there was the *Arno*, and if she was indeed deserted and they could save her, it would be a small fortune for every man in the *Langdale*'s crew.

Cam knew all about this, for the word 'derelict' had often cropped up in the lazy dog-watch yarns during the voyage, but the law and what it might mean to him and the rest of the crew was far from his mind as he watched the battered *Arno* lift and swing, lurch and dip in the ceaseless Atlantic swell. The hard grey light across her revealed the crushed ventilators in her wells, the twisted rails along her sides, the shattered lifeboats hanging from the davits amidships; these things told the story of the battle that had been fought and lost; and the sea breaking across her decks as she dipped and rolled, roared sullenly like a wild beast guarding its prey. What Cam was seeing, and perhaps Andy too, was the chance of snatching it away, of taking up the fight that unknown crew had yielded and beating the sea, in spite of the advantage it had gained.

Would Captain Carey take up the challenge? That was the question in everybody's mind and there was never any doubt about the answer. Nevertheless, when at last he dropped the glasses and swung round on the mate with the order to clear the starboard lifeboat, a little cheer went up from the waiting men as they broke away and scrambled up on to the boat-skids.

The plan was to board her, make fast the heaviest towline the *Langdale* could devise, and tow her stern first into the nearest English port which was Falmouth.

It was a tricky business getting a boat out in such a sea, and dangerous too. One small miscalculation, a single moment of carelessness, would be enough to smash her to matchwood against the ship's side and leave the men who were in her fighting for their lives in the broken water. But old Andy knew the sea and small boats and he made no mistake. First, to lighten her, the boat was cleared of all its gear except the oars; then she was swung out and the painter passed forrard and made fast on the fo'c's'le head with a man standing by to let go when he got the word. Calamity, Taffy, the bosun, and Cam jumped in and took their places on the thwarts – the bosun at stroke, Cam at bow, and the others in between. Andy followed and looked around.

'Two more men!' snapped Andy and, without a word, the carpenter and another sailor swung over the gunwale; then Andy shipped the steering oar and stood balanced in the stern sheets. 'All set?' he shouted. 'Okay then, lower away!'

Quickly the boat dropped and with Calamity and Taffy fending her off, Cam and the bosun stood by to cast off the falls. The moment she was waterborne they unhooked and while Andy dragged deep at the long steering oar, Cam hove with all his strength on the painter. The boat surged ahead, swinging on a wide curve away from the ship's side, and when she was well clear the mate bawled out the order to let go the painter and they were away. Then, working swiftly, Cam coiled down the painter and taking up the bow oar added his weight to the rest.

Captain Carey had brought the *Langdale* as close as possible to the *Arno* and to windward of her, so her bulk made a lee for the boat. Pulling hard, with Andy standing on wide-spread legs aft, the steering oar bending like a bow in his powerful hands, they crossed the wild gap between the two ships almost as easily as if they had been in dock; then faced the problem of getting aboard the *Arno* and making fast to her.

They were under her lee and that meant they were saved the full force of the sea, but the swell remained, and one moment they were deep in the trough, with the derelict towering dangerously above them, the next on her crest, looking down on the rusty decks.

But old Andy had already made up his mind about it. From an outswung davit on the high midships structure, a boatfall dangled in the water and, as the lifeboat swooped towards it, he sang out to Cam to boat his oar and stand by.

'Grab that fall, Cam, and shin up it, then throw us a line.'

Cam swung his oar inboard and, facing ahead, waited. For a moment he thought the sea would swoop them out of reach of the fall, but, just at the right moment, Andy pulled on the oar, and the sodden rope dragged across the bow of the boat.

Reaching up as far as he could Cam gripped, then, with a queer empty feeling inside, jerked himself into the air and started to climb. He was keyed up with excitement and could feel the power of his arms and legs as he swarmed up the fall in a series of swift pulls right to the davit-head; and there he came to the really dangerous spot, for it was necessary to transfer the weight of his body from the vertical swinging fall to the almost horizontal curve of the rigid davit.

It would have been a clever piece of work in a gymnasium but there, hanging over the side of a plunging ship in mid-Atlantic, it needed not only skill and strong arms, but guts as well. Pausing a moment to steady his breathing, he gripped the fall with his thighs and ankles and, stretching to the limit, reached up swiftly with both hands and got them round the davit; another pause while he carefully tested his hold, then he pushed off from the fall and hung for an instant by his hands as his body swung through the air. At that moment the *Arno* lurched deep to starboard, dipping the edge of her deck plates under all along and making him feel he was diving head first into the sea. But he kept his grip and, with another powerful jerk of his body, coolly swung his legs up and round the davit.

He was safe then, and breathless but unhurt he slid along the dripping metal bar and dropped on to the deck.

After that it only took a few seconds to make a coil of the end of the boat-fall and heave it across into the *Langdale*'s boat where Taffy bent the painter to it.

Cam pulled in the line and, unhitching it, ran aft along the derelict's decks to make it fast to a bollard.

With the line secured like this, it was comparatively easy to control the movements of the lifeboat. Calamity took the steering oar and, after easing her in close enough for Andy to jump on to the *Arno*'s well-deck, swung her out and held her riding at a safe distance.

Then the mate and Cam made a swift tour of the abandoned ship, but their search told them nothing. The log-book was gone from the bridge and the safe in the captain's room gaped wide open and empty.

'They left in a hurry all right,' grunted Andy, pointing to a half-eaten meal on the saloon table, 'but they stopped long enough to take her papers with them. Come on, son. We can look round more thoroughly later. The main thing now is to get a tow-rope aboard and make it fast.'

He led the way out on deck again and, changing his husky whisper for his special deep-sea roar, called the boat alongside again so the carpenter and Calamity could join them on the derelict. The boat was then cast off and with the bosun holding her head up to the sea, drifted down to leeward where the *Langdale*, having steamed in a wide circle round the *Arno*, was waiting to pick them up.

Meanwhile, on the poop of the derelict, Andy explained the plan. He proposed to rouse out the heaviest wire the *Arno* carried and, laying it double round the coaming of her after hatch, pass the ends through the hawse-pipes just forrard of the poop, then bring them back on deck. When they got the *Langdale*'s line aboard they would shackle it to these ends and the wire would then form a bridle.

'Got the idea?' he snapped.

Calamity shook his head. 'I don't see why you want to tow her stern first. It's just making things awkward. Seems to me the simplest thing is to unshackle the anchors, make the tow-line fast to the cables, and tow her head first. Length is everything towing in a seaway and there's a hundred and twenty fathoms of cable to play with that way.'

Andy nodded. 'True enough, but she's deep down by the head. So deep, her fore-deck's awash beyond the foremast. That would make her tend to tow under, and no line would stand the strain.'

'And,' put in the carpenter, 'there's that hole in her side.

She's floating partly because of the cargo that's in her, but also because the bulkhead in number two hold is still standing. There must be a big strain on it and towing ahead would increase it.'

Calamity admitted he had overlooked these factors.

'Okay then,' said Andy. 'Let's get going.'

They set to, but, though they went all out on the job, over an hour was passed before the wire was arranged to the mate's satisfaction. Then they turned to the task of getting a line aboard from the *Langdale*. Cam had thought this would mean another boat trip and when at last he had time to look up and take stock, he was amazed to see Captain Carey had already hoisted the lifeboat up again. True, it was still swung outboard and stripped with the painter passed forrard, but there was no one around it and he wondered how the linking of the two ships would be managed without it.

He was quickly enlightened.

Steaming slowly ahead the *Langdale* swung once more round the derelict and, when she was dead to windward, stopped and drifted slowly down until she was as close as she could safely come. Then she was held there with the engines just turning over and a lifebuoy fastened to a heaving line dropped overboard with such clever judgment, it drifted right into the *Arno*'s side.

It was a simple job then to fish it out of the water with a boathook and, with the link-up made, the rest was a matter of sweating and hauling. The heaving line was made fast to a two-and-a-half-inch manilla, and when this was in their hands Andy's little crowd bent it to the ends of the wire bridle they had made and gave the signal to heave away. The winch on the poop of the *Langdale* rattled and clattered, and as it drew the wire aboard, the ends were stoppered off and shackled on to the waiting tow-rope.

The men worked quickly but it all took time and it was close on noon before they were finished, and after a last check up Andy signalled for Captain Carey to go ahead.

Then slowly, and with infinite care, the *Langdale* moved away to the full length of the towline and took the strain. Those first few minutes were the most important of all, for the derelict was stopped and would be a dead weight on the line. Once she was moving again there would be a certain amount of springiness, but until then a single jerk might part the wire like a rotten thread.

Breathlessly the men on both ships watched. They saw the line lift out of the water and grow taut; they watched it shedding a thin spray as it twanged and vibrated under the strain. Then suddenly it sagged again and for a moment it seemed as if the *Langdale* was backing up; but the beat of the engines went on and at last the waiting men realized it was the *Arno* that was moving.

Calamity's long face split into a triumphant grin. 'We've done it, young Renton,' he yelled, slapping Cam on the back. 'We've got her and she's under way!'

But old Andy shook his head. 'Don't crow yet, Calamity. We've a long way to go and I don't like either this sea or the look of the weather. That line's carrying a tremendous strain every time she plunges.'

So through the afternoon they watched the towline with anxious eyes, and between whiles swept the horizon to windward where the cloud formations had merged into a lead-coloured mass that seemed to become darker and more menacing with each hour that passed.

When he saw that everything possible had been done, Andy went off to complete his exploration of the derelict. He made it very thorough this time and was all of an hour and a half on the job. The engine-room especially seemed to keep him a long time, and when he finally left it and rejoined Cam and the rest on the poop the excited gleam was back in his eye.

'Anything fresh, sir?' asked the carpenter.

The mate shook his head then jerked it forward like an old turtle. 'Not a thing. But –' He stopped.

'But what, sir?' prompted Calamity.

'But she's a diesel-engined job and everything seems in order down below. I'm just wondering –'

At that moment the towline parted. They heard the twang of it as it came clear of the water and simultaneously the rounded stern of the *Arno* dipped and plunged into the face of the swell. This added strain was too much for the already overloaded wire and once more the *Arno* was helplessly adrift – this time with nightfall close on them and the weather threatening to break any minute.

The situation was desperate, but Andy had foreseen it and already a new scheme, hazardous and daring, was working in his mind. It hung on the fact that the *Arno* was a diesel-engined ship, not a steamer. She needed no firemen and could be worked with an engine-room crew of three – two even at a pinch if they were tough enough.

While the *Langdale* picked up the broken towline and manoeuvred close again, he put it to the group on the poop.

'It won't be easy, mind,' he warned. 'There'll be little sleep for anybody and we'll have to live on hard tack all the time. Then we'll never know about that bulkhead forrard. We could tow stern first, but under her own power I reckon we'll have to go ahead and chance it. We'll try to shore the bulkhead against the pressure first chance we get, but even so it might go at any time and, if it does, it's good-bye *Arno*. She'll put her head down and slide under without warning and maybe we'll all go with her. But it's the only way. There's another gale brewing up and we wouldn't be able to hold her even if we had proper towing gear. It's either that or abandoning her again. Are you game?'

Calamity spat over the rail. 'I'm aboard her now and I'm staying as long as she floats. You can count on me, mate.'

'And the rest of you?'

'That goes for me, too,' said the carpenter.

'And me!' said Taffy and Cam together.

Again old Andy grunted. 'Then everything depends on us having one engineer aboard the *Langdale* who knows something about diesels. Besides him we'll need one of the juniors to stand watches with him and a good fireman, or maybe the donkeyman, to spell them. Then on deck we'll manage with two in a watch but we'll want another mate to relieve me. I'd like the second but doubt if the skipper will part with him; but we'll see.' He swung round on Cam. 'Can you semaphore?'

'Yes, sir. I got a lot of practice in at it with Rusty at Cardenas.'

'Good. Then away with you on to the top of the chart-room and get your arms wagging. I'll be right behind you to tell you what to say.'

Cam raced off amidships, dodging a couple of seas as he crossed the well-deck and, picking a good stance clear of the standard compass, began to make the calling-up signal to the *Langdale*.

There were plenty of eyes aboard her fixed on the *Arno* and by the time old Andy had hoisted his stocky body up beside Cam, Rusty was in position on her chart-room top and making the answering signal.

When Cam said he could semaphore he was making no idle boast. Both he and Rusty were experts but, even so, it took a long time to pass across all that Andy had to say – his opinion of the prospects, his suggestion for taking the *Arno* into port under her own power, his minimum requirements in men to do so, and finally his urgent appeal to Captain Carey for permission to try the venture.

Then there was a long pause while the skipper consulted with the chief engineer, the two mates, and the rest of the hands. To the group on the derelict this pause seemed endless. They had already decided and were impatient for the issue to be settled.

When at last Rusty wagged 'Okay' daylight was already waning and every one knew it would mean fast work to transfer the extra men and get the boat back to the *Langdale* before darkness shut down on them.

It was a near thing, but they managed it, and while Calamity and the others gathered in the galley for a much-needed meal, the third engineer dived below with his gang to give the engines the once-over.

By a lucky chance he knew the type well, and was quickly up on deck again to tell Andy he was ready to start when he got the word.

Leaving the rest of the skeleton crew to finish their meal, Andy and Cam made their way to the bridge, each of them clutching an enormous sandwich of bully beef between two slabs of bread. Cam took his place at the wheel and tried it over and, when he was satisfied the steering gear was in order, passed the word to Andy.

'Steering gear's okay, sir!'

'Right!' said Andy. 'Here goes!' and, drawing a deep breath, he swung the engine-room telegraph to slow ahead.

It was a breathlessly exciting moment, waiting for the dead forsaken ship to come alive again. Would she respond? Did the third engineer really understand that enormous machine in the heart of her?

So much could go wrong even now and they might so easily have miscalculated. Tensely they waited as the seconds ticked by, hearing the sullen swish of the sea in and out of the wound forrard and the loud beating of their own hearts. Then, when the suspense had become almost unbearable, there came the loud explosive hiss of compressed air from the engine-room, a rattle, a series of thumps which quickened then eased into the steady beat of pistons, and the throb of the propeller under the stern. At the wheel, Cam felt the life come into her as she picked up way.

'North-east is the course!' cried the mate, and Cam swung the wheel to fetch her up on to it.

'North-east it is, sir,' he shouted.

Then there was a cheer from the hands clustered round the galley door, and an answering shout coming faintly down wind from the *Langdale*.

The hazardous bid to save the *Arno* had begun.

16

IT was just on six o'clock in the evening when the battered *Arno*, snatched from the hungry sea by the mate of the *Langdale* and his skeleton crew of six grim-faced, determined men and one tough, excited boy, came up out of the trough of the swell and steadied on a course for the Scilly Isles.

The fight was on and, though it had been a strenuous day for all of them, there was no thought of resting. The derelict was manned; she was under way and the white wake showing faintly luminous in the gathering darkness astern showed she was steering well; but there was still much to be done.

At the moment all their doubts and fears were centred on the bulkhead at the after end of number two hold. This wall of thin steel plates was one of the several built athwart the ship to divide it into compartments, and it alone held back the water pouring in through the gash in her side, and prevented it surging aft to flood the engine-room and sink her like a stone.

It had to be strengthened and, leaving the third mate in charge of the bridge, with Calamity at the wheel, old Andy led the rest of the deck crowd below to see what could be done.

As it happened, there was plenty of heavy timber in the 'tween-decks, and while the mate selected the most suitable pieces and helped the sailors and Cam to lower it into the bottom of the small auxiliary boiler room just forrard of the main engine compartment, the carpenter, who had already rooted out some tools, was busy measuring and sawing.

They put everything they had into the job, and when at last after three hours' hard driving Andy cried enough, the bulkhead was crossed by a series of three-inch planks laid horizontally and wedged into position by great square baulks from the edge of the deck plates.

Carefully the old mate tested what had been done, tapping with a hammer here and there.

'Good work!' he said in his husky whisper of a voice. 'Now if only we can do something with that hole in her side I'll feel more comfortable. But we can't tackle it in the dark. We'll get going on it as soon as daylight breaks.'

Then weary, but easier in their minds than they had been since boarding the *Arno* that morning, they climbed back on deck and gathered on the bridge to work out a few important details before settling down for the night.

The question of watches was quickly disposed of. They would start from midnight with Andy, the carpenter, and Taffy; till then the third mate would carry on, with Calamity at the wheel, and take over again at 4 a.m. with Cam as third man. This arrangement would give the boy the extra couple of hours' sleep he sorely needed.

'About sleeping,' Andy said when this had been settled, 'I reckon we should all stay amidships as close to the bridge as possible so as to be handy in case anything busts loose. I'll kip on the chart-room settee myself and the rest of you had better use the cabins on the lower bridge. That's the lot for now, I think, so let's get our heads down.'

The men clattered away down the ladder, but Cam did not go immediately in spite of the weariness that ached in every bone and sinew of his body. Instead he watched the mate move across into the port wing of the bridge and slowly followed him. Always he had been powerfully drawn towards this squat silent man, and even when the two of them were at odds on the outward passage there had been, deep down inside the lad, a warmth and liking he couldn't destroy. And now day by day he was knowing the mate better; with knowledge was coming first respect and then understanding that grew unnoticed as a strong link between them. Because of this, Cam knew now that behind the wooden, expressionless face, the set mouth, and hard, unblinking eyes, Andy was worried.

They had embarked on a dangerous venture and while the risks were the same for them all, when everything was said and done it was Andy who carried the whole crowd. It was his responsibility and Cam was suddenly seeing him, not as a tough old shellback, but as a fellow human being who was terribly lonely. He wanted to give the mate a feeling that he wasn't alone any more, but to do it either by word or gesture was beyond him, so he just stood there silent at his side staring with him into the darkness across the unseen tumbled sea.

They stood there together for a long time, then at last Andy sighed and broke the silence.

'Well, Cam, what's on your mind?'

Cam flushed in the darkness. 'Nothing, sir. I was just thinking what a terrific day it's been.'

'And how rosy everything looks, eh?'

'Well – yes, sir, in a way. We've got her under way; we've shored the bulkhead, and now –'

'And now we've only got about fifteen hundred miles to go to Falmouth and it's all plain sailing.' Again Andy sighed heavily. 'I wish I could feel it was. That's a devil of a lot of ocean, Cam, in any sort of ship, and in one crippled as the *Arno* is –' He broke off and pointed ahead to where the stern light of the *Langdale* showed like a fallen yellow star. 'That's our big hope. So long as she can keep us in sight we'll be okay whatever happens, but if we lose touch there'll be nothing to fall back on but our own guts and will to win through.'

Cam stared at the light. It seemed very small and far off, and sometimes it disappeared altogether for a moment or two as the *Langdale* pitched easily over the heavy swell.

'If we could count on the weather holding it would be simple,' Andy went on, almost as if talking to himself. 'But it won't. It was banking up to windward when the daylight failed and the glass has been falling steadily ever since. Better get below now, son, and grab some sleep. There'll be another heavy day tomorrow.'

So leaving him there, a short vast shadowy figure under the gathering storm wrack, Cam went down and, in spite of all his aches and the excitement that still kept him tense, he was asleep the moment his head touched the pillow.

When he came on deck again at 4 a.m. old Andy was still on the port wing of the bridge, still staring out into the darkness, and Cam knew, without being told, he had been there throughout the night.

Taffy gave Cam the news as he handed over the wheel. The weather had broken just before midnight, the wind coming away out of the south-west and rapidly reaching gale force. The wind itself was fierce enough, but it was accompanied by blinding rain squalls which cut down visibility to a few hundred yards and lashed the wild running sea constantly higher.

At 2 a.m. old Andy, fearful of the growing strain on the crippled ship, had turned her round and hove to, stern on to wind and sea. It was a desperate manoeuvre that called for all the skill and nerve, all the instinctive understanding his long experience of the sea had given him.

And when it was done they had lost the *Langdale*'s winking light. The very first squall had blotted it out for them, but Taffy caught another glimpse of it in a slight lull just on two bells. He lost it almost immediately and they hadn't seen it since.

They never did see it again, the *Langdale* either, and when the grim grey day broke on a wind-torn empty ocean, Cam knew what Andy feared most had happened. They had lost contact and were on their own, fighting now not only for the *Arno* but for survival.

Andy led them to it. He was magnificent, hard as iron, tough as steel and indomitable; and in the days that followed Cam often thought of what Captain Carey had said after the adventure in Boca del Sol.

'There's more to it than that, Cam. There's being able to make decisions and carry them through; there's being able to keep your head when things bust loose; there's improvisation; and, most of all, there's being able to hold your crew together behind you, and keep them fighting and believing in you when hunger and cold and the savagery of the sea has left them with nothing to hang on to but that belief.'

He saw it now and understood as he hadn't done before and day by day he learned and grew.

They got busy on the hole in the side as soon as there was light enough to work by.

First of all, Andy, with a line round his middle and a man standing by ready to drag him back if he slipped or the leaping sea licked him away, surveyed the damage; then, gathering the hands round him on the bridge, he reported and outlined his plan.

The unknown, colliding ship had run head on into the *Arno* and the impact must have been terrific. It had buckled the deck plates and driven a huge dent deep into her side before finally penetrating the shell plating.

'But,' Andy went on, 'It might not be so bad as it looks. For one thing, the actual hole is straight up and down; for another, the bows cannot have penetrated the side very deeply. Perhaps they came up against something pretty solid in the cargo and that took the impact. I don't know, but anyhow although there's the dent and the vertical gash with the ragged edges of the torn plates turned in, the hole's nowhere more than a few inches wide.'

'So far as you can see, that is,' put in Calamity.

Andy nodded. 'So far as I can see; but I should say it would get narrower the deeper it went.'

'That may be,' said Taffy, 'but where does it get us?'

'I'll tell you,' Andy answered; then with the glint of excitement in his eyes but the same set face and quiet husky voice he explained.

If they could rig something reasonably pliable, but at the same time heavy and solid enough, down the length of the gash and outside it, the pressure of the sea itself would force it against the opening and seal it. That would reduce the amount of water coming in to a quantity the pumps could handle.

Calamity was on the idea like a flash. 'By crikey, mate, you've got it,' he cried. 'A grass rope would do it if there's one aboard, and if we could get a good strong tarpaulin stretched under it when it's in place she'd ride as dry as chip.'

Andy squared his shoulders. 'I don't expect anything as wonderful as that. It might not even work at all; but if it does and we can get some of the water out of her forrard and keep it in check I'll be satisfied.'

After a brief search the grass rope they needed was found under the poop. It was as thick as a man's thigh and about ten fathom – sixty feet – long. A great heart-shaped metal thimble was spliced into each end of it to form an eye. When he saw it and tried the weight of it, Cam wondered how they would ever get it from the poop on to the fore-deck; but the carpenter, who was still searching, presently turned up with a coil of two-and-a-half-inch manilla and a couple of queer-looking pulleys with hooks on them called snatch-blocks. With these and the power of the deck winches they set to, and by breakfast time had the huge rope where they wanted it – across number two hatch, right in line with the gash.

The next thing was to get the line passed from the deck, over the port side, right under the ship's bottom and back up the starboard side on to the deck again. As this would have to carry the weight of the grass rope and hold it in place against the drag of the sea when the ship was under way again it had to be good, and Andy spent a long time examining various wires before he finally decided on a practically new two-inch warping wire which was wound on a reel on the fo'c's'le head.

Running the free end of this along the port side they shackled it to a ring-bolt in the deck, then unwinding a good length from the reel dropped the wide loop it now formed over the bows clear of the anchors. When it had slid out of sight down the stern-post, they hauled it aft down the starboard side, slipped it into a snatch-block hooked on to the hatch-coaming opposite the holed shell plates, and carried it back to the winch by the foremast.

Two manilla lines were passed in the same way, then the carpenter, who was still rooting about in the bosun's locker, unearthed a brand-new hatch tarpaulin which they folded lengthways to give four thicknesses of canvas. When the folds had been nicely flattened out, a stout line was fixed to each corner and all the gear they needed was ready.

During all this time the gale had howled and shrieked around them, and though the *Arno* was riding easier, with her stern to the sea, she was so far down by the head, her foredeck was continually awash. This meant they were working in water sometimes waist deep. That, with the cold and the tremendous effort involved in handling the huge grass rope with so few men, had left them almost exhausted, but Andy gave them no respite.

'Keep going, boys!' he said over and over again. 'It's neck or nothing now and if we ease up we'll stiffen and never get started again.'

But at the same time he watched them carefully and nursed them all he could. Somehow he seemed to be everywhere and whenever anyone slipped or stumbled his hand was there to steady him; with an uncanny instinct he anticipated each threatening sea that boarded and robbed it of its menace. Cam marvelled at his power and drive, and wondered a little fearfully how much longer he could last, but through all that day saw no sign of flagging in him. The hard, expressionless face seemed to tighten hour by hour, the rims of his cold ice-blue eyes grew red and sore for want of sleep; but he went on and the boy was warmed with a fierce pride in the thought that he was with such a crowd and such a leader.

No time was wasted on eating. The spare man of the engine-room crew kept a pot of coffee going on the galley stove and served mugs all round every hour or so. Then at midday there were slabs of corned beef in hunks of bread. They ate huddled in the lee of the midships structure, and the moment their hands were empty went to it again.

The success of the scheme depended on getting the weight of the hawser against the tarpaulin so it would be forced into the gash before the sea could get hold of it and rip it away. This made it a tricky job that needed fast work and perfect co-ordination from everybody once the canvas was launched over the side.

So the next step was to double the great grass rope back on itself to bring the eyes at either end together, then to lash them securely to the hatch-coaming. When this was done and the end of the wire running under the ship's bottom had been shackled to the bight, that part was ready and they turned to the tarpaulin, making one end fast to the stanchions under the twisted bulwarks and bending the stops at the other end on to the manilla lines coming up from under the keel.

All the lines were drawn up taut and Andy made a last careful check up.

'All set,' he said, then, standing by to guide the tarpaulin over the rail, he gave the word in his great bull voice. 'Haul away!'

Laying back at the signal they pulled madly with every ounce of strength they possessed; the canvas slid down the battered shell plates smoothly as oiled silk, and when the last inch of slack had been taken up they stopped off the lines. Then, crossing the hatch, they began to ease the grass rope over the bulwarks with their shoulders, while Calamity at the winch kicked the stop-valve wide open and got all the power possible on the twanging wire.

It was a chance in a thousand and it came off. The hawser slid into place over the tarpaulin as smoothly as that itself had gone over the shell plates. There was still the possibility that the sea would tear it loose, or the straining of the ship widen the gap so it drove through into the hold; but for the moment at least they had succeeded in filling the perilous breach and, with luck, it would hold.

And now, while the third mate took over the wheel, the whole crowd gathered for a while in the galley to get the chill out of their bones, then went below to strip off sodden clothes and get some sleep against the black night that lay ahead – all of them except Andy. He went down to the engine-room to report progress to the engineer and persuade him to get the pumps going all out on number two hold.

When Cam turned out again with Calamity at four o'clock in the afternoon and went on to the bridge, he knew at a glance Andy's idea was working. Already the *Arno*'s bows were riding higher, and under the beat of the main engines he could hear the powerful throb of the pumps still throwing out water from the flooded hold.

'Where's Andy?' he asked as he relieved the third mate at the wheel.

'On the chart-room settee. Kipping at last, but I've orders to call him at eight bells.' The third mate stood down from the grating. 'Looks like we've got it by the tail now. If it keeps on fining away like this, everything will be rosy by morning; then he reckons on opening up that hatch and getting a cement box and some shores over that hole on the inside.'

Cam whistled and his eyes gleamed. 'That'll mean shifting some of the cargo, won't it? Bit of a job with a skeleton crew.'

'I know, but he'll do it. Brother, Andy's taking this hooker into Falmouth and nothing's going to stop him. He'll swim there with it on his back if all else fails.'

And it did seem then as if they had got on top of things. Even the weather seemed to be turning in their favour. The wind had eased and though the sea still ran high it was truer and put less strain on the ship.

But the sea is implacable; it never gives up, and as if it knew and understood what was in their minds, it waited and struck again when they least expected it – not at the ship this time but at the second most important of their desperately in-adequate crew.

The weather continued to improve during the night and the next day broke shining clear on a sea that was flattening out with every hour that passed.

So much of the water had been pumped out forrard that she was now only slightly down by the head, and except for an occasional crest surging through a wash-port as she rolled, the fore-deck was dry. Andy decided to open up the hatch and try to consolidate the gain they had made in sealing the gap the previous day.

They started before breakfast and at eight o'clock the third mate was due to go down the hold and relieve old Andy to eat. They never knew what happened. Like all of them he was numb and shivery for want of sleep and that makes a fellow uncertain on his feet. He stumbled at the head of the bridge-deck ladder and pitched into the well-deck.

Cam found him there and yelled for the mate who came tearing up out of the hold. 'Don't move him!' he warned, then went down on his knees and made a swift examination with his great banana-like fingers. When he had finished he stood up and stared across the sea.

'Is he badly hurt, sir?' asked Cam.

'Right leg broken, just above the knee. He'll be all right.'

'But that means –'

'Yes, I know. That means he'll be on his back for weeks and we're left with five hands to work a crippled ship over fifteen hundred miles of the Atlantic; five hands and only one of them qualified to take charge of a watch.' For a moment his broad shoulders sagged, then he flung them back and, clenching his great fists, turned to the unconscious man at their feet. 'But,' he said slowly, and somehow just because his voice was quiet his words seemed to carry more weight. 'But we aren't done yet. Call the hands, Cam.'

17

AFTER the first shock of finding the third mate at the foot of the bridge-deck ladder, old Andy seemed to take the accident in his stride, almost as if he had foreseen it and prepared a plan to meet it.

The first thing was to do everything possible for the injured man.

Getting him up the steep ladder out of the well-deck into the shelter of the saloon was a problem quickly solved. Under the watchful eye of the mate he was lifted on to a hatch-board, lashed securely to it, then hoisted up and carried along.

He was still unconscious when they set him down on the deck of the saloon, and with Calamity and Cam standing by to pass the things they needed, Andy and the carpenter between them soon had the broken leg set and splintered.

Coming to almost immediately they had finished, the third mate looked down at his bandaged leg and groaned his dismay.

'Suffering snakes, mate! I've made a mess of things now all right!'

Andy patted his shoulder. 'That's okay, son. We'll get along. How's it feel?'

'Oh I'm all right.' The third mate's voice was impatient. 'But what about the ship? How –?'

'Leave that to us.' Andy stood up. 'You lay back and make your mind easy. That's the best way you can help us now.' His voice was quiet and confident then, but a few minutes later, when he had gathered the remainder of his weakened crew round him in the wheelhouse, Cam again caught the sharp note of anxiety in it.

'There's no use blinking the fact, boys,' he said. 'This puts us in a nasty jam. It's been tough going up to now but all we've done so far is going to seem like a picnic against what lies ahead.'

Calamity spat through the window. 'We know that, mate; but let's have it. We can take it.'

'Right, then. First of all the watches. We're down to five men including myself. My idea is, Calamity and Cam for one with Calamity in charge; Chips and Taffy for the other with Chippy in charge; and myself standing by for both so I can take over if anything heaves in sight day or night, and between whiles spell whoever happens to be on. That way Taffy and Cam won't grow roots through the wheel grating. Is that agreed?'

The two sailors and the carpenter nodded. 'Agreed!'

'And you, Cam?'

Cam hesitated. His eyes were fixed on old Andy's face and he was thinking how easy it all seemed – too easy. 'Agreed, sir,' he said at last, 'but –'

'But what?'

'That's only part of it, isn't it?'

Andy grunted, then sighed heavily. 'Yes, only part of it and maybe the easiest. There's the third mate. We can't leave him on his own down there night and day. He seems okay just now but he must be badly shaken and he's liable to get brooding and go scats if we don't look after him. There should be somebody with him all the time but I don't see how we can manage it and work the ship too.'

Cam frowned, then suddenly his face lit up. 'Look, sir. You'll need to be on the bridge all the time, ready to take over when anything comes along, but couldn't the rest of us make our beds up in the saloon and eat down there too? Once we've got under way there'll always be one of us off watch.'

'True enough!' agreed Andy. 'I hadn't thought of that.'

'True enough until something else busts loose,' growled Calamity.

'Well, anyhow, it will do to be going on with,' Andy snapped, and for the first time since they had boarded the *Arno* there was a note of impatience in his voice. He stopped speaking and his keen blue eyes swept round the little group; then he went on in his usual husky little whisper of a voice. 'That brings us to the last thing, which is the most important of all. Before we do anything else we've got to finish the job we started this morning.'

For a moment the three men looked at each other in amazement. It seemed to them the loss of the third mate had changed the whole outlook. They had taken it for granted that all ideas about strengthening the repair to the gash in the ship's side would now be dropped, and the strength and energy they had left concentrated into an effort to get the ship into port in the shortest possible time and before any of them cracked under the strain.

Andy gave them no time to protest. 'I know what you are feeling about it,' he went on quietly. 'The weather is fining away; the sea's going down; time is the one thing that counts any more, and you think we should get cracking while the going's good and there's still enough of us left standing to drive her.'

'That's the way I see it anyhow,' put in Calamity. 'We've something like fifteen hundred miles to go, and I reckon it will take us all of twelve days to make it if the weather holds. We'll all be at the end of our tether by then, so for Pete's sake let's get under way and get it over.'

'Twelve days – if the weather holds!' Andy went on. 'That's

just it. And if the weather doesn't hold it might be fifteen or twenty days; and if it comes away again really bad it might be –'

'Curtains!' said Cam.

'Exactly. Well, I want to make sure it isn't curtains whatever the weather does and to cut it down to eight days if it stays good. It's not an easy decision to make and it will be tough going to carry it through. Just because of that, I want you to understand what's in my mind and why I've made it.'

Then briefly he went over the arguments for and against and, as he listened, Cam recognized in him one more quality a real seaman must have – the ability to think ahead, to weigh a number of things one against another, and see them as they really are and not as he would wish them to be.

The weather was fining away, but it was the season of the equinoctial gales, and the weather signs – even the barometer – were good for only a few hours ahead. The ship was crippled. They didn't know how long the plug they had got over the torn plates would stay in position, and even in a smooth sea it would be dangerous to drive her at as much as five knots. The moment she started to pitch or roll heavily again, they would be forced to heave to or go on at the risk of the gap widening and the sea sweeping in on them again.

If, on the other hand, they carried out the original plan, it would mean losing another day before getting under way; but with the damage shored and tied inside and a cement box over it, they'd be able to lift her bows still higher. This would lessen the strain on the whole repair. In a smooth sea it would be safe to drive her then at eight or even ten knots; and if the weather did break again, while it would be necessary to ease her down, they could carry on for much longer before heaving to, and, what was most important, they would be more confident of her staying afloat.

Against such sane, quiet reasoning, there could be no argument, and after arranging for the spare engine-room hand to fix up meals and keep an eye on the third mate, the work on number two hold was resumed.

All through that day they worked, using all the tricks the experience of the men had taught them or that the quick wits of Cam could devise to save their own strength and spin out their power to endure.

First the cargo in the square of the hatch was broken out and dumped over the side. It was mostly big pitch-pine logs and by mid afternoon they were down to the 'tween-deck. Then the snatch-blocks came into the picture again as the stuff along the port side was dragged out into the space they had cleared.

Andy was everywhere at once, it seemed, and Cam struggled desperately to keep up with him, one minute levering the butt of a log over the edge of a deck plate with a handspike, the next flinging his whole weight against it to guide it clear of a stanchion, or squeezing himself through a tiny gap to hook the sling round another.

Handling heavy timber is dangerous work under the best of conditions, and there, in a crippled ship rolling in a seaway, it needed strong nerves and real guts. They took terrible risks but, except for Andy, who tore his hand slightly with a rag on a wire sling, they came through it unscathed.

When darkness shut down, the great cargo lamps Andy had already rigged were switched on and the work continued in their hard white glare right through the night.

At seven o'clock they were through to the torn plates, but another two hours passed before sufficient space had been cleared around them and the damage itself could be tackled.

If any of the men had any doubts left about the wisdom of Andy's decision, they were finally dispelled at the first sight of the hole from the inside. The great grass hawser had plugged the gap all right and, with the raising of the bows, a good deal of the damage had been lifted above the water line; but, low down, the sea was still squirting in along the ragged edges of the plates, and it was plain to see how easily and quickly all they had gained could be lost again.

Andy's plan was first to strengthen the breach with ties of steel rods running across it and bolted to the vertical frames on either side; then to stop the leak with oakum and build a strong wooden casing or box over it which they would fill with cement. The oakum would hold the water back long enough for the cement to set and then, with the box securely shored and stiffened against any strain that might come on it, it would hold.

It was a long job, and when at last Andy declared himself satisfied, the new day was already greying the eastern sky.

How they got the hatch covered and battened down when they were finished, Cam never knew. He was out on his feet and conscious of nothing but a dull throbbing ache all through his body, his eyes were sticky and sore for want of sleep, and his feet felt as big as balloons. Somehow he dragged himself up the ladder and into the saloon to flop on to the settee. Then the black waves of sleep he had been fighting back so long, surged up and swamped him. He didn't hear the clang of the telegraph nor the beat of the engines in response to it as the *Arno* at last got going and picked up speed; and he didn't hear old Andy come into the saloon shortly afterwards, nor feel his great hands as they pulled off his seaboots and straightened his legs.

A whole minute the tough old shellback stood there looking down at the exhausted boy, then covering him over with a blanket he went soft-footed back to the bridge.

The *Arno* drove on and when Cam woke she was already a

good hundred miles nearer Falmouth, for somehow Andy had managed to keep going through the whole day, and thus made it possible for the lad to sleep the clock round and come back on deck fit for anything that might turn up.

The routine of watches was set going that night and, though the long tricks at the wheel were wearing, everything went easily for a while. The wind veered to south-west and fell light, and gradually the sea went down until it stretched smoothly from horizon to horizon with never a white-cap in all its expanse and only the long Atlantic swell's slow movement to disturb it.

The nights were still and full of stars, and all the hazards they had dared, the tremendous efforts they had made, slipped into the background of their minds like old half-forgotten yarns.

In two days they knocked off just under five hundred miles.

'Four more days at this rate,' croaked Calamity when the mate gave them the distance run that noon – 'four more days and we'll raise the Scillies. It's all over bar the shouting.'

But that night, at eight bells in the second dog-watch, old Andy called Cam into the chart-room. He was bending over the table, and the moment the lad saw the grim face harshly lit in the light flung back from the white chart, he knew they were up against it once more.

'You wanted me, sir?' he said quietly.

For a moment Andy didn't move and gave no sign that he had heard, then suddenly he swung round and shot a question.

'You did a fair bit of swotting at navigation while we were round the islands, didn't you, Cam?'

Cam hesitated. 'Well, yes, sir.'

'And you know the feel of a sextant in your hand?'

'There's one in my room in the *Langdale,* sir, and I messed around with it a lot in Cardenas Bay but never worked up any of the angles I shot.' Cam saw now Andy's face was grey with pain. 'Anything gone wrong, sir?'

The mate sighed. 'Plenty, and to spare. Take a look at that.'

He thrust out his right hand and Cam gasped. The huge fist was swollen to almost double its normal size, and the wrist, usually so bony, was puffed as big as the calf of a man's leg.

'Remember I jagged my hand on a wire that day we were working down the hold? Well, it was hardly more than a scratch and I thought nothing of it. But now it's gone septic – poisoned. I've done all I could to check it and keep the use of my hand, but it's got away on me and I reckon by tomorrow I won't be able to hold a sextant or lay off a course on the chart. That means we're finished, Cam, beaten by a miserable scratch after all we've come through, unless –' He stopped.

'Unless what, sir?'

'Listen, son. I've watched you ever since you boarded the *Langdale* in Liverpool and I've seen everything you've done and I've learned a lot about you – more maybe than you know yourself. I've watched you go ahead, run off the course and lose your bearings; and I've watched you find them again and get back under your own steam. I was glad to see you tumble into the boat that morning we boarded this old scow, and I've been glad to have you with me since, glad I didn't send you back. But all the time I've worried about you.'

'But why, sir? I'm tough and –'

'I know, but you're young, and it's bad to put too much strain on a young growing body.' Again old Andy paused and pulled at his lip with his left hand, then suddenly his head shot out from his shoulders. 'What did you think of the re-arrangement of watches we made when the third mate was crocked? Didn't you feel that as an apprentice you had some sort of claim to his place?'

Cam flushed and shuffled his feet. 'No, sir. I just knew that you would decide what was best for us all.'

'Well, I did; and I seriously thought of putting you in charge of a watch, but if too much physical strain is bad for a youngster, too much mental strain, too heavy a responsibility is worse, and it was for your sake I decided against it.'

'And now –'

'Well, what do you think? It's your hands and your eyes I want. I could check everything you did except your sextant readings and course lines.'

It was only then Cam really understood what was in old Andy's mind and still for a moment or two he couldn't believe he was hearing right.

'You mean you want me to help you with the navigation?' he stammered, and Andy's cold eyes softened at his bewilderment.

'Put it that way if you like. You're our only hope now and if you don't feel up to it, all we can do is to carry on till we sight another ship and get help from her – another officer to take us into port. Are you game to try?'

Cam flushed. 'If you'll trust me, sir. With you behind me I feel I could do anything.'

Andy smacked his good hand down on the table and his shoulders straightened as if a load had suddenly been lifted from them. 'Right, then. Call the hands and we'll put it to them.'

So presently, when the little group of unkempt sea-worn men had again crowded into the wheelhouse, he explained the new trouble that had overtaken them and his plan for overcoming the difficulty.

'I'm not going to try to persuade you either way,' he said. 'You know the lad; you've worked with him and stood watch and watch with him. So far he's measured up with the best of us, but he's young and it's up to you. What's it to be?'

Before any of the others could speak, Calamity thrust himself forrard. 'Look mate,' he growled, 'we set off – you and Mr. Carter and the rest of us – to take this old wreck into Falmouth, and, by crikey, we're going to do it and ask nobody's help. We're sailormen – not a bunch of blooming farmers – and young Renton is one of us, so what's all the argument about? You're crocked – all right, let's get on with what's left to us. That's my opinion and that's what all of us feel.'

That was, beyond any doubt, the proudest moment Cam had so far lived, and though it was the beginning of a desperately anxious time which tried him to the limit of his power, he would not have forgone what followed for anything.

Through all the next four days and nights he thanked his lucky stars for the hard work he had done in Cardenas. Even with that behind him and the solid background of knowledge it gave him, the practical business of navigation came all strange and new to him and without it he would have been lost.

Andy was a tower of strength. Somehow he seemed to know instinctively just when help was needed and how to give it, and as the days wore on and the *Arno* reached nearer and nearer to the mouth of the Channel, Cam found himself drawing closer still to the old sea-dog and marvelling that they could ever have been at loggerheads.

Although the injured hand gave him great pain, he never complained, but was always gentle and understanding and, what was perhaps most important of all, he did everything he could to make Cam sure of himself.

That was the boy's greatest difficulty – lack of confidence. It wasn't that he was afraid, but untried and inexperienced, and it was a big responsibility he carried; big for an established shipmaster; frightening for a lad not half-way through his apprenticeship.

The problem was to raise the Scilly Isles, establish a position off them, then from there to navigate past Land's End and round the Lizard to the pilot station outside Falmouth. As a starting-point, the position in which the *Langdale* had first sighted the derelict was practically useless, for after the two ships had parted company, the *Arno* had drifted about for two full days. However, at the beginning of the fine spell Andy had worked up a position and checked it continuously until he crocked up, so at first glance it seemed a simple matter to steer straight from that point to Scilly, but there was more to it than that.

First the compass. A magnetic compass doesn't point to the true north but to a point some distance from it called the magnetic north, and the pull of the magnetic pole changes slightly from place to place and time to time. This change is called variation, and this was the first thing Cam had to allow for when he was working out a course to steer.

But magnetic variation is only one of the complications. All iron and steel structures have a certain amount of magnetism in them, and a ship, being mainly built of steel, is always pulling the compasses to one side or other of magnetic north. This is known as deviation and while it varies for every course, it is also liable to change from one day to the next.

Cam had to allow for this and, even after the course was worked out, go on checking it twice a day with a bearing of the sun at sunrise and sunset to make sure the ship was really keeping to it.

Then, along the thousand miles still to go there were unknown currents and drifts. It was easy to work out from the rate the engines were turning what speed she was making through the water; but at one time she would have a current with her helping her along; and another time it would be against her, holding her back, one day it would set her east, the next day west and, because of this, what she made through the water was one thing and the distance she actually covered over the ground something quite different.

This distance run could only be accurately worked out from 'sights' – observations of sun and stars – from which the exact latitude and longitude could be calculated.

The sun was the main thing and surest. At nine each morning they worked out their longitude from it, and at noon the latitude, Cam using Andy's sextant to get the angles, then working them up under the old man's eye.

Andy's big worry was that the clouds banked along the horizon would reach up and overcast the sky. This often happens, and for days – sometimes weeks – a ship runs blind and has no exact knowledge of her whereabouts. With a long sea passage ahead it doesn't matter a great deal if the sun is obscured for a while. An approximate position can be calculated from the speed of the engines with allowances for wind and sea. This is called 'dead reckoning'. Sooner or later, on a long run, the weather will clear, and then with reliable sights to go on, the dead-reckoning position can be checked and the course corrected. But no navigator likes to make a landfall on dead reckoning and, because of this, morning longitude and noon latitude weren't enough for Andy. He had Cam taking double latitudes in the afternoon, the latitude from the pole star in the evening and more star sights in the early morning.

In that short time Cam came to know the night sky like the back of his hand. The constellations like Orion, Tauri, Cassiopeia, the Plough, and the planets such as Venus, Saturn, and Jupiter, became real things to him and their movements the one certain factor in a world that was a waste of treacherous shifting water and deep hidden menace.

But, as if the crippling of Andy had been its last desperate attempt to defeat their purpose, the sea continued calm. Driving on, the *Arno* steadily cut down the distance still to go; the patch on her side held, and though the men became haggard with the strain and red-eyed for want of sleep, they stuck it out and there were no more accidents.

On the fourth day after he had taken over from Andy, Cam shot the noon sun as usual, worked up the position, and laid it off on the chart. Then he picked up the dividers and measured the distance run.

'Two hundred and forty-five miles I make it, sir,' he said, turning to Andy. 'That's the best we've done yet.'

Andy grunted. 'And what's the distance to go?'

Carefully, Cam measured again. 'A hundred and fifty-eight.'

'That's to the Bishop Rock lighthouse itself, eh?'

Cam nodded.

'Well then, the light is visible in clear weather eighteen miles off. That gives us a flat hundred and forty to go till we raise it. But there'll be the Channel tides. Look 'em up, Cam, and give us a time.'

Cam turned back to the table and made some more calculations. 'Four o'clock in the morning, sir,' he said at last. 'That is if my sights and figures are right and the weather holds.'

'The weather might do anything, but I'll swear by the sights. We'll raise her all right but we'll get the pole star this evening, just to make sure.'

As it happened, however, that shot at the sun was the last sight they got, for in the middle of the afternoon the cloud banks spread across the whole sky, and by nightfall Cam was in a sweat, going over his figures, checking course and distance, time and the tide, over and over again, and all the time wondering if he had overlooked anything or slipped up somewhere.

Andy sent him below at eleven o'clock. 'Go and get some

sleep, son, and don't worry. I'll call you about six bells in the middle watch, just in case we've run a little ahead.'

Cam went but, weary as he was, he couldn't sleep, for the moment he closed his eyes he saw the chart and the closely printed columns of the navigation tables; and the figures danced and whirled in his brain and wouldn't make sense.

He was back on the bridge again just before 3 a.m. The night was black as pitch but calm and there wasn't a thing in sight. Standing with Andy in the port wing, he stared and stared ahead for the first blink of the light which alone now could prove all he had done.

Presently, Calamity at the wheel beat out eight bells and the blackness ahead was still unbroken.

'Wait, Cam!' whispered Andy. 'Be patient.'

But as the minutes passed the tension in the boy grew, and all the faith and confidence he had in himself oozed away. Again his mind picked up the figures and all the time now the question beat in his brain: 'Where did I go wrong? How have I slipped up?'

Then at half-past four he stiffened, and his swinging stare steadied. A light – right dead ahead. A minute he stared, with his heart beating fast, then he sagged again and groaned. The light was there but it was fixed – a steamer's masthead light and beyond it the darkness was still unbroken.

'Steady, lad!' said Andy. 'Give her time.'

'But it's getting on for five now and we should have raised it an hour ago.'

'I know, I know. But the log isn't absolutely reliable and we might have had a stronger set than we reckoned on. I've checked your figures. Be patient.'

'But if my sight was wrong – if we've set to the norrard or if –'

Andy snorted. 'If pigs had wings and –' Suddenly he

187

stopped and gripped Cam's arm with his good hand. 'Look, what did I tell you? There she lifts, two points on the port bow just as you reckoned.'

For a moment Cam could see nothing, then he caught the double blink in the blackness, and as he lost it again, began to count.

'One, two, three, four . . .' His voice trembled a little with excitement as he measured off the time. A double flash every fifteen seconds was the characteristic of the Bishop Rock light and this was the final test. Would it blink again at the right interval, or was it just the stern light of another steamer upping over the swell?

'Thirteen, fourteen, fifteen.' And there it was again.

Cam relaxed and leaned against the dodger. The *Arno* had made her landfall.

18

THE rest was easy.

With the Bishop in sight, Cam brought the *Arno's* head round to starboard on to the new course he had already worked out, and drove on for the Lizard.

The distance was forty-nine miles and when the new day broke they could already see the dim loom of the Cornish coast like a mauve mist ahead.

At ten in the morning the white octagonal tower on the cliff top was plainly visible and he hauled her up again for Falmouth Bay.

Half an hour later they saw the black-hulled yellow-funnelled pilot cutter standing out towards them, and with a little sigh of relief Cam rang the engines down to stop.

The men on the cutter stared curiously at the great grass hawser hanging over the side, and when the pilot came aboard and stumped up on to the bridge he was bubbling with excitement.

'Well, well, captain,' he said as he shook hands with old Andy, 'you're the last packet we ever expected to see in Falmouth Bay.'

Andy grunted. 'You heard about us then?'

'I'll say we did. The *Langdale* docked in Liverpool three days ago, but she wirelessed the story the night she lost you and you've been headline news ever since. That skipper of yours — what's his name?'

'Captain Carey.'

'That's right. He swore you'd get her home but nobody

believed him. They've had salvage tugs out and half the ships in the Atlantic watching for traces of wreckage from you, and here you are, large as life and cool as kiss me hand. How did you do it?'

Andy's tough old face broke into a smile, and he waved his hand to Calamity and the rest. 'Ask them,' he said. 'They aren't very pretty to look at, but they're seamen.'

The pilot stared, then noticed Andy's slung right hand. 'That may be – but you yourself – you're crocked. Where's your mate?'

Andy's good hand reached out to draw Cam forward, then slid across his shoulders. 'This is him,' he said quietly. 'Tough as old boots, keen as mustard, and guts to spare. In all my days I never sailed with a better one.'

Cam flushed and grinned awkwardly at the pilot. He was all in, too tired to think or care about anything except that the harbour was in sight and they had beaten the sea; but the mate's gruff praise warmed him and seemed to make all the hardship and struggle worth while.

That kept him going until the ship was safely moored and he had seen old Andy and the third mate off to hospital; then he rolled into his bunk, let go everything, and took his fill of sleep.

He woke to find the mate back on board and in command again. The injured hand had been properly dressed, and though it still needed a sling and a lot of care, inside a week it would be completely healed.

There was still much to do, but Andy had a way with other people beside sailormen and he managed to get the deck hands and the engine-room crew on their way to rejoin the *Langdale* next day. Cam and he followed forty-eight hours later when all the formalities and urgent legal business arising out of their great achievement had been completed.

They arrived in Liverpool after an uneventful railway journey and for the second time in three months Cam walked along the dock wall looking for the *Langdale*; but now there was confidence in his stride and eagerness in his face. He had found his lost road and knew that nothing would ever turn him from it again.

These are other Knight Books

SOUTH SEA ADVENTURE
Willard Price

Commissioned to bring back a collection of dangerous sea creatures, Hal and Roger Hunt sail for the little-known islands of the West Pacific in a chartered schooner. They have an additional errand; to visit and examine the pearl-oyster beds of a secret lagoon, and it is this which brings them into the greatest danger – greater even than capturing a huge sea-bat, or weathering a hurricane.

Ask your local bookseller, or at your public library, for details of other Knight Book, or write to the Editor-in-Chief, Knight Books, Arlen House, Salisbury Road, Leicester LE1 7QS